UNUSED PERFUME

Unused Perfume

ANGEL MARTINEZ

BROADMAN PRESS
Nashville, Tennessee

DEDICATION
To *Mary Lillian Stewart,*
A treasured friend

© Copyright 1982 • Broadman Press
All rights reserved
4251-89

ISBN: 0-8054-5189-7
Dewey Decimal Classification: 252
Subject heading: SERMONS—COLLECTIONS
Library of Congress Catalog Card Number: 81-70908
Printed in the United States of America

Foreword

It was with delight that I learned Dr. Angel Martinez was preparing to issue this volume of sermons. He is so gracious to grant me the privilege of writing a brief word of commendation concerning it.

Dr. Martinez is an ardent, careful student of the Bible. He believes and loves it with a passion, and he proclaims its truth with power and evangelistic fervor. He is a homilist of the highest order, one who presents an ageless message with freshness which challenges the mind, delights the heart, and motivates the will.

He has dedicated his life to the work of an evangelist, and the blessings of God have attended his efforts. He relies not upon sensational methods but upon the power of the Holy Spirit. It has been this writer's privilege to have him as the preacher in five revivals. He returns again and again with a renewed challenge to large congregations of hearers.

Adept at using illustrations which illustrate, yet the abiding strength of Dr. Martinez is seen in his strong reliance upon the Scriptures. I have never known a preacher who cites more Bible passages. He is at home in the Scriptures, having committed all of the New Testament and most of the Old Testament to memory, but most of all he has committed them to his heart.

These messages are some of the cream of his preaching. These sermons are a challenge to adult minds, yet their simplicity will also appeal to the minds and hearts of young people and children.

Knowing the author as I do, I commend *Unused Perfume* to all who would draw from it devotional reading and sermonic gems for one's own proclamation of the message of God.

HERSCHEL H. HOBBS
Pastor Emeritus
First Baptist Church
Oklahoma City

Introduction

The true revival sermon is homiletics on fire. The flame must burn successfully and consume the indifference of the saint and the indecision of the sinner. This frozen generation needs to be defrosted. We cannot afford to have icicles in the pews and an iceberg in the pulpit.

The purpose of evangelism is to get the church out of the church. The issue is not how many souls you are winning to Christ; the crux of the matter is how many people are the people you have won winning? God help us to make our faith portable.

The sermons contained in this book were lifted from the field of battle, and I present them in their spoken form. One sacrifices literary preciseness in a venture like this, but the intent of the proclamation is to persuade the listener to "kneel at the foot of the cross."

ANGEL MARTINEZ

Contents

Foreword by Herschel H. Hobbs
Introduction by Angel Martinez
1. *Unused Perfume* (Mark 16:1,6) 11
2. *A Man for All Seasons* (Matthew 11:28-30) 21
3. *The Biography of a Believer* (Acts 11:26) 31
4. *Wait on the Lord* (Isaiah 40:31) 42
5. *We'll Work Till Jesus Comes* (1 Samuel 16:11) 54
6. *Something Beautiful* (Romans 10:1-4) 65
7. *All in the Family* (Luke 16:19-31) 77
8. *Guess Who's Coming to Dinner* (Revelation 3:20) ... 89
9. *Honey in the Lion* (Judges 14:8,9) 99
10. *Does Jesus Care?* (Acts 9:4; Luke 10:41; Luke 22:31; Matthew 23:37, 27:46) 109

1.
Unused Perfume

And when the Sabbath was past, Mary Magdalene, and Mary the mother of James, and Salome, had bought sweet spices, that they might come and anoint him. And he saith unto them, Be not affrighted: Ye seek Jesus of Nazareth, which was crucified: he is risen: he is not here: behold the place where they laid him. (Mark 16:1,6)

On a beautiful Sunday morning, the first day of the week, three wonderful women came to the tomb to anoint and perfume the body of the Lord whom they loved. Two Marys and Salome had spent the previous day securing these expensive fragrances to lavish on the dead body of the Savior.

As they approached the tomb they wondered how they would enter it, for they knew that a great stone was blocking the entrance. Their strength would not be equal to the task. But when they arrived, to their amazement, the huge stone had been rolled aside, and when they entered the sepulchre, they saw a young man dressed in white sitting on the right side. They were terrified, but the heavenly visitor reassured them and then informed them that the Christ for whom they sought was not there. He even showed them the place where He had been laid. Jesus of Nazareth had arisen from the grave and had become the firstfruits of them that slept.

The three women did not get to use their spices and perfume. The Lord Jesus was not there to receive their thoughtful ministrations. The fragrances were not used. And leaving the historical beauty of the resurrection, I want to concentrate upon that perfume. It was not used. And often this is the case in life. We do not use the perfume of life. We have it, like these women had it, but it remains bottled up. God wants us to spread the fragrance of our lives on others. I think that the poet said it beautifully:

> Do you know the world is dying,
>   For a little bit of love?
> Everywhere we hear the sighing,
>   For a little bit of love.
> For a love that rights the wrong,
>   Fills the heart with love and song,
> They have waited Oh so long
>   For a little bit of love.
>
> From the poor in every city,
>   For a little bit of love,
> Hands are reaching out in pity
>   For a little bit of love.
> They have burdens hard to bear,
>   They have sorrows we must share,
> Should they falter and despair,
>   For a little bit of love?

Every child of God carries a fragrant scent peculiar to him. But so many of us keep it bottled up; we do not share with others. We let the cares of this life or preoccupation or inherent apathy and indifference inhibit the blessing that we could be to others every day. And then time goes by, and we have not been to others, for the glory of God, what we could have been. Oh, how we fail people around us by not sharing ourselves, our love, our kindness, our enthusiasm. And every one of us has those qualities and use them sparingly. If only we could realize the power within us that could be unleashed in a world that is suffering because of the lack of this concern for others. The world is not impressed with our budgets and buildings or even our morality and goodness. If we are going to capture the world for Jesus, we will have to open the bottle and let the perfume of our lives radiate in the home, at school, and in the place of business.

You see, when you give yourself away to others, it is a way of saying that you care. A journalist who was fond of the talented author, Sinclair Lewis, studied his literature and wrote favorable reviews about it. One day he had the opportunity of having an interview with the man whose work he admired. During the interview the journalist conversed with Lewis about his significant works. He expressed admiration for his novels, such as *Babitt* and *Main Street*, in which Lewis had so cleverly reflected the moral failures and hypocrisy of our times, but the famous author was cold and unresponsive. He seemed to love crowds and adulation but he cared nothing for people.

I. The Fragrance of Fun

When I speak of the fragrance of fun, I am not referring to something light or spurious. I am describing the inner radiance that God gives to believers at the point of salvation. The child of God has a peculiar joy that the Lord bestows because he knows that his name is written in heaven, that he has the presence of Christ in his everyday living to face the problems of existence, and that at the end of his earthly sojourn he steps into the presence of the Heavenly Father, for to be absent from the body, is to be face to face with the Lord. This kind of joy can be contagious, and it can encourage others to accept Christ so they, too, may experience this "joy unspeakable and full of glory."

Harvey Cox, a Harvard theologian, in his book *Feast of Fools*, has emphasized this brand of inner radiance as being a part of our evangelism. He contends that unless we reproduce the gladness and inner happiness that characterized the early Pentecostal church, we are not going to impress our contemporary culture. He affirms that the world is not impressed with our buildings. The world of business and pleasure have beautiful buildings. They will not be impressed with our budgets; the world of finance and entertainment spend great sums to advance their product. They are not even impressed with our morality. If we say that we do not drink or smoke or do this or not do that, this does not attract the attention of our humanistic society. Many of their devotees do not drink or smoke and lead exemplary lives for reasons of health and plain cosmetic concern. But if we could recapture the radiant joy that sent the church into spiritual orbit, we could make an impact on our time.

In 2 Corinthians 6:10 Paul gave a beautiful description of this inner composure of the Christian when he said that the Christian had nothing and yet possessed all things. This is a marvelous description. For as the devil says to the believer, "I am going to give you something," the Christian can reply, "You cannot give me anything because I possess all things." If, on the other hand, the devil says to the child of God, "I am going to take away so and so from you," the believer can reply, "No, you cannot because I do not have anything." It is that inner victory which gives the Christian life a fragrance that must be shared with others.

We are living in a lackluster world. Despite the fact that we are loaded down with conveniences, and gadgets of all sorts abound in profusion, there is a perennial discontent that dominates our current culture. There is a great need for God's people, who are more than conquerers, to share themselves with others and reflect the inner joy of Christ and dispense it to a confused civilization. This inner malady which abounds in our world is reflected in Byron's sad lament:

> My life is in the yellow leaf
>   The fruits and flowers of love are gone,
> The worm, the canker, and the grief,
>   Are mine alone.

And there is no excuse for this mood. Our country has been blessed profusely; but it seems that pleasures and affluence have not dispelled the inner gloom. This is a victory that must be won on the inside, and it seems that human beings touching each other can do more to encourage this achievement than mere material things or salutary conditions.

That is why comedians are so loved in our day. We pay them high salaries to make us laugh. We want to enjoy life, and most of us don't know how, and those of us who know the way have insulated ourselves and become an island. This is not the teaching of the Word of God. We should share what we have and what we are. That is why Jesus lived for others. He knew the contagious effect of love, joy, and peace, so he fraternized with publicans and sinners. And when he was criticized for his associations, he informed his retractors that the sick need a physician, not the well. If we are going to follow Jesus and emulate his example in our lives, like leaven in the bread, we need to involve ourselves as Christians in the midst of the world's despair and try to share the inner happiness that Christ has given us with the world around us.

Jesus was a radiant person, and the circumstances around him were not the type that induce joy and happiness. But he won the victory on the inside, and he shared it with others. The artists of the past have always depicted him as a somber and sad person. I do not believe that this is the case. People do not gravitate to that kind of person, and Jesus, according to the Gospels, was a winsome individual. Publicans and sinners hovered around him. Little children ran to meet him when they saw him coming. I believe that he smiled, laughed a lot, and had a sense of humor. The epistle of Hebrews declares that he was anointed with "the oil of gladness." Even on the cross, the Word of God declares that Jesus, "for the joy that was set before him," endured the cross, despising the shame.

Judson, the great missionary, on one of his furloughs was asked by the reporters if it were true that the people everywhere were comparing him to the apostle Paul. He replied, "If that be true, I am sorry this is being said; I do not want to be like Paul, I want to be like Jesus." And I want to be like Jesus, who carried this inner joy and shared it with people around him. He left the fragrance of his joy everywhere. That is why the Scriptures say that the disciples were glad when they saw the Lord. And to be a Christian is to be like Jesus. The word "Christian" is two words; one is Greek, *Christ*, which is Messiah, or the One sent from God. The other is Latin, *ian*, which means a follower of someone, like the Herodians were the followers of Herod.

And believers should be perennially happy, not only because of what they have, but because of what they *don't* have. A Puritan divine said that the miseries we *have not* are a blessing we have got. I know that there are many problems in your life, but have you ever thanked God for what you don't have? You don't have cancer, you don't have tuberculosis, you don't have blindness, and the like. Let us not ignore the blessing of not having many miseries that afflict the human race. Let us learn in whatsoever state we are, therewith to be content. And let us not bottle up the perfume because everything is not perfect. You can decide to choose to be radiant, and this will become infectious to every person you meet, and they will be better off for having rubbed shoulders with you for a little while.

II. The Fragrance of Friendship

Here is another essence that is so important and can be shared with others. In the Roman epistle, Christians are commanded to be hospitable, "to be given to hospitality." We make friends by being aggressive, by entertaining others, and keeping our doors open to their solitariness and needs. Karen Horney, the great psychiatrist, in one of her books contends that there are three things we can do with others. First, we can move against them. This is the technique of the psychopath, the criminal. We can hurt other people and try to destroy them. Second, we can move away from them. We can become, as they say in psychiatry, schizoid. In other words, we can become loners, and withdraw from others and refuse to fraternize with them. Third, we can move toward them in kindness, love, and helpfulness. She contends that, for our own sake and for others, we had better adopt position number three.

And the child of God should take the initiative in friendship relationships. In other words, he should make the first move and proceed to nourish the relationship by not waiting for the other person. Jesus told his disciples that he was sending them into the world as lambs among wolves. Usually, the wolves are the aggressors, and the lambs are the passive ones. Jesus is asking that we reverse this and that the lambs be the aggressors and make the move toward the wolves. This is a revolutionary concept, but he practiced this with the woman at the well and others, and he bids us to follow in his steps.

Friendship, aside from being a wonderful blessing and delight to the person, can also have many useful functions to the believer. You can win someone you know to Christ. A total stranger cannot have the rapport with a sinner that a friend can have. And if the fragrance of friendship should be used for no other purpose than this, it would justify its careful cultivation by every child of God. Friendship builds a bridge between two people and gives an opportunity for witnessing and restoration. The unsaved man appreciates the friendly spirit of the Christian more than he appreciates his morality, personality, or excellence. Sinners are lonely. They need the love and concern of Christians. And the child of God should be mindful of this and should always be doing his best to cultivate this quality with others, in order to capitalize on the opportunity of saying a helpful word to the unbeliever.

Jesus was a friend of sinners. He received them and ate with them. He was not parsimonious with his time or sympathy. Friendship takes time and thought. The little lady who was instrumental in winning me to Christ, and consequently my entire family, first built a strong tie of friendship and then used it as a fulcrum to introduce us to the grace of God. No stranger, visiting casually, would have had much influence on us. But this neighbor who had learned how to love and care had an access to our situation that ultimately brought our salvation. We were stubborn at first, and we are indebted to her persistence that brought us to the foot of the cross. Jesus was that way. When Judas betrayed him with a kiss, Jesus called him friend. In other words, he was saying to Judas, "It is not too late; you can still repent. The door is still open; the clock of divine grace never strikes twelve."

Robert Louis Stevenson, in his book, *Travels with a Donkey*, said that "the best things we find in our travels through the wilderness of this life world is an honest friend. We travel indeed to find them. They are the end and the reward of life." So if friendship assumes that high category, it should behoove every believer to be on the lookout for friends, both for his own sake and for the cause that he represents. These friends can be a help in the hour of sorrow. Many of us never know how many friends we have until the hour of difficulty descends.

But our friends can also rejoice with us in the great moments of our lives. You recall that when the shepherd found the lost sheep, he called together his friends and enjoined them to rejoice with him on having found his possession (Luke 15:6). And in the same story, when the woman found the lost coin, she invited her friends and neighbors to celebrate with her over the retrieval of the piece of silver (Luke 15:9). When Jesus healed a man, and the man wanted to travel with the Lord, the Savior encouraged him to return to his home and tell his friends, and share with them the victory that had occurred in his body (Mark 5:19).

We should never let anything destroy friendship. Don't let friendships die. Fight for them. Sometimes careless words can damage friendship. And when a close companion says something caustic, we want to fight back. People who fight fire with fire wind up with ashes. I have often heard people say that they were going to give so and so a piece of their mind. I wouldn't be that generous with anybody. Keep your inner fragrance at any cost. When people sin against us, we can learn from the different ways which were used in the story of the woman caught in adultery (John 8). We can employ Moses' way who commanded that the sinner be stoned. We can use man's way—to expose them, as the men in the story told Jesus that they had caught the woman in "the very act." Or we can use the Master's way, forgive them, and say to them, "Neither do I condemn thee: go, and sin no more."

So let's not withhold the fragrance of friendship. Let us unleash it upon the world. Friendship may be the Christian's greatest evangelistic thrust. Touch somebody. You have a personality that can reach people no one else can.

III. The Fragrance of Faith

The inspired writer said that faith is the victory that overcomes the world (1 John 5:4). By "the world," he did not mean flowers or stars or rainbows, but rather the world system that embraces worry, fear, and guilt. And these mental states are not limited to the poor and the sinful; they enfold the world of natural man, whether he be poor or rich, famous or infamous, educated or illiterate. This is primarily what God looks for in man primarily. The writer of Hebrews said that without faith it is impossible to please God (Heb. 11:6). God is pleased with our good morality, our spiritual activities such as prayer and going to church and scriptural stewardship, but nothing pleases him more than our faith. We please him when we can look up into his face and trust him, even though there are problems, heartaches, and sorrows in our experience. We please him when we can say with Job that though he slay us, yet will we trust him. This is what glorifies him. He is looking for faith; Jesus asks us, when he comes again, will he find faith on the earth (Luke 18:8)?

If we possess saving faith and also the faith to confront life's difficult situations, we are to share these with people around us. This fragrance that is so essential to effective living should not be bottled up. And yet, sad to say, many believers who possess these qualities insulate themselves and refuse to pass them on. We share this faith with others when we allow it to dominate our experience. When we practice faith in the midst of storms, this affects others. We set an example for those around us which will help them emulate our faith. No man lives to himself, and no man dies to himself. We are constantly affecting others by what we do and what we don't do. When we believe and manifest faith and trust in God, we initiate a chain reaction that will have benefits beyond our comprehension. When we are negative, we infect our friends and others with the spirit that will compound defeat.

We share our faith with others when we encourage them. There are so many defeated people in our day. The pressures of life are not easy to bear, and we are encouraged to bear one another's burdens and so fulfill the law of Christ. One can see discouragement written on the faces of people. I see discouraged mothers who have fought the battle to rear their children in the way of truth, only to be broken by detours of the young people that contradict everything parents have taught them. I see businessmen, harried by the competition of our feverish culture, defeated and discouraged. I see it written on the faces of young people who seem to have lost their way in a world that reduces individuals to ciphers. When we encourage others, we are opening the bottle of perfume; we are sharing our faith with those who need it.

We share our faith with others when we comfort them. Paul said that God has comforted us in our tribulation so we might be able to comfort them who are in trouble with the same comfort that God has given us (2 Cor. 1:4). So there is a double function to comfort. When the Lord comforts us, we are to share it with others. God has promised to walk with us in the valley of the shadow of death. When his presence is realized in our experience, and we feel the touch of his healing hand, our task is to apply that truth to the troubles of others, not to keep it to ourselves. When the lepers of Samaria found food outside the besieged camp, they returned to the famished city and shared the tidings (2 Kings 7:9). So when the Lord confers on us the blessing of comfort, we do wrong when we keep it to ourselves.

Let us not be selfish with divine blessings. The world is in dire need for someone to build a bridge between God's grace and the need of man. Let us share the fragrance.

2.
A Man for All Seasons

Come unto me, all ye that labour and are heavy laden, and I will give you rest. Take my yoke upon you, and learn of me; for I am meek and lowly in heart: and ye shall find rest unto your souls. For my yoke is easy, and my burden is light. (Matthew 11:28-30)

If one could travel up and down America, knock on every door, feel the pulse of the people of our land, and catch the moods of every citizen in the home, at work, and in the school, I believe one could summarize the American feeling in one word, "Unrest." We are living in a restless society.

Everyone is tired—the rich and the poor, the educated and the illiterate, the good and the bad are all victimized by the feeling of unrest. On the human level, there seems to be no cure for this malady. Despite the fact that we are well-fed as a nation, and we have an abundance of education, pleasures, and sports on every hand, a television set in nearly every home, and conveniences that do our hard labor, we are still the most exhausted society in human history.

Jesus faced this mood in his day. If you read the first part of Matthew 11, you will find that even John the Baptist, of whom Christ said there was "none greater," was having moods of despair and defeat. So this feeling is not restricted to a certain segment of society. Even the spiritual people can be afflicted by this malady. In the same chapter (verses 16-19) Jesus describes the people of his day as being fractious and unpredictable. Nobody or nothing could please them. They were like children who could not decide what to play. If someone suggested they play music and dance, they refused to do that. If someone else suggested that they play a sad or serious game, they were not in the mood for that.

Then Jesus began to upbraid the cities for manifesting the same perplexity in their response to the word of God. They were sated with divine revelations that had been given to them in abundance. The Lord reprimanded them for being so obtuse. If the word revealed to them had been delivered to Tyre and Sidon, they would have repented in sackcloth and ashes. Therefore, they would be more responsible than the less fortunate nations who were not privileged to hear the divine offer of salvation and deliverance (verses 20-24). To these confused believers and common people and wayward, ungrateful cities, Jesus addressed the significant word that they come to him and find rest. What they could not find in their pleasures, wealth, education, or even within themselves, they could find in him. And to these ungrateful metropolises, the Lord is inviting, "Come unto me." Nothing can be as destructive and fatiguing as ingratitude. And then Jesus focused upon the individual, with his multitude of problems and difficulties, and invites him to find rest—not in things—but in Christ.

Jesus is the answer. His love, forgiveness, and daily guidance are the remedy for our day. But so many think that this is a simplistic answer. Surely, it must be more complex than that. How can a person who lived two thousand years ago have a solution to the pollution of our modern day? But it works. Those of us who have tried it, although we cannot understand its mechanics, have found the way of Christ adequate for the hour of sorrow, for the hour of failure, for the hour of confusion, for the hour of despair. He tells us in our text that we are to come to him, and he will give us rest. Notice in verse 28: he *gives* us rest, and in verse 29, we *find* rest. The given rest is the rest of salvation and forgiveness; the found rest is the rest of sanctification or Christian growth because we serve him when we take his yoke, and we learn of him as we watch him operate in every area of human living. But both rests come through Him.

There is no human situation that can baffle the grace of our Lord. His power is sufficient for every problem we face. He is a man for all seasons. It makes no difference what difficulty you are confronting in the present moment; if you come to Jesus for help and for wisdom, he will give it to you freely, and he will not upbraid you or turn you away. He said that he is the way, the truth and the life (John 14:6). He is the way—without him there is no going; he is the truth—without him there is no knowing; he is the life, without him there is no living. His physical life and his atoning death and his victorious resurrection make him eligible to help us and to give us rest.

I. Come to Jesus When You Are Glad

Jesus is equal to all of the seasons of the soul. Man passes through many experiences, but in all of them, he finds no surcease, no peace, until he anchors the ship of his life in the harbor of the Savior. You recall the amazing story of the wedding at Cana. Jesus and his disciples were invited, and the mother of our Lord was also in the group. When this unnamed couple was contemplating the people to invite to that festive joy, their wedding, the list of guests included Jesus and his followers. This was commendable, to invite Jesus to a wedding. So many of us wait until the difficult hour, the hour of stress and storm, before we come to Jesus. We think that he is not interested in our festivities, in our joys. Not so with this Cana couple; they wanted Jesus there, and we should remember that the Lordship of Christ covers the totality of life, not just a segment of it.

Life is made up mostly of hours that are light and devoid of stress and difficulty. To exclude Christ from these is to exempt him from the most of life. But he belongs in every area of our living. That is why David, the bard of the Old Testament, could walk through "the valley of the shadow of death" and testify that the Lord was walking with him in that dark hour. But immediately he turned from the gloom and the shadows of life and declared that God prepared a table before him and anointed his head with oil and overflowed his cup. These were customs of the day; these were the expressions of joy and happiness. David affirmed that the Lord is present in the festive situation, as well as the funeral and the sorrow. Let us not forget this great truth, and come to Jesus when life is going smoothly and well.

We need him in the light hour because some of the greatest temptations can assail us when the sun is shining, and the sky is blue, and the rivers flow gently. Most of us are moral when we are sick, and the allurements of the flesh are of no consequence when there is sorrow and despair. But in the happy hour, the life of man can turn to folly and iniquity. The devil likes to monopolize leisure time. Our generation is highly tempted at this point. Our fathers were better people than we are, not because they were better intuitively, but because they were too tired to misbehave! Their work and toil were arduous and fatiguing as they labored in an agrarian culture from sunup to sundown. When night fell, they were ready for bed—to sleep. Not so with our generation. We are allowing the machine to do our manual labor and permitting the computer to do our thinking, so we conclude the day with extra hours. It is at this point that Satan can move in with devilish whisperings and induce us to deviate from the path of righteousness. These surplus hours must be filled with the presence of Jesus, who is concerned that we be glad and rejoice, but not to use our leftover time to destroy our character and hurtfully influence others, and bring dishonor to the Lord.

We must remember that his Saviorhood includes the whole of life. He came to give us life and to give it to us more abundantly. Abundant life is the result of his saving power. We must not think that salvation operates only in the realm of sin; it is concerned with the biggest part of our life: our joys, our blessings, our gains. The devil knew this, and so he tried to dissuade Jesus from being a Savior. In the wilderness of temptation (Matthew 4), he tried to get Christ to turn stones into bread. Jesus informed him that he did not come to earth to be a baker, but a Savior. Again, Satan tried to get Christ to jump from the temple and attract attention. But Jesus reminded the devil that the only sign he would give this generation would be the sign of Jonah. He would be someone that would come from below, like Jonah came out of the whale, not one who would jump from above.

So many of us want to use religion and the Lord as a spare tire, only for an emergency. But emergencies are intermittent—they come at long intervals. The Lord wants us to fill in the empty spaces with his presence and guidance. So we need Jesus when the sun is shining, and the sky is blue, and the grass is green just as much as when the storm clouds gather. We need the Lord when the cheek is red, and the step is firm, and the eye is clear just as much as when sickness comes, and we must go under the surgeon's scalpel. We need the Savior when our loved ones are around us, and everyone is prospering, and health abounds in the family just as much as when death comes to a member of the home, and crepe hangs on the door, and we make our tearful way to the city of the dead. Come to him when you are glad.

II. Come to Jesus When You Are Sad

Not only are we to come to him in the sunny hour, but we need to come to Him when every star has gone from our sky. He is a man for all seasons. He is equal to our troubles. And troubles and heartaches are going to come to all of us sooner or later.

Joseph, that pure young man of the Old Testament, was maligned and thrown into a pit. Daniel, that brave hero of the past, was cast into a lion's den because he had been faithful in prayer to God. David, the sweet singer of Israel, walked in the valley of the shadow of death. Absolom rebelled against him; one of his sons had committed incest with his sister; another son in the family slew his brother. David had all kinds of trouble. Peter was in prison for preaching the good news. Paul suffered shipwreck, was beaten with rods, and stoned at Lystra and left for dead. John was banished to the lonely Isle of Patmos. Catherine, the beautiful Scotch Christian, was thrown into the sea; McKal, the missionary, was sent to the scaffold; Latimer, a devout Christian, was burned at the stake, and Jesus went to a cross.

When Mary and Martha faced the dark hour (John 11), they sent for Jesus. Lazarus had died. He was a close friend to the Savior. Jesus came to the grave and wept. So Jesus is available when our hearts are broken. And remember that God will accept a broken heart, if you bring him all of the pieces. When troubles come, our loved ones and friends can offer their condolences and maybe help in some elementary way. But no one can mend a broken heart like Jesus. His constant presence has been promised. He will never leave us nor forsake us. He will walk with us in the valley of the shadow of death. Some of you who read this today have had an overwhelming sorrow. There is a vacant chair at your table. A loved one has departed, and you are trying to adjust to the vacuum that they have left in your life. No one can take their place, but Jesus has promised to give us comfort and insight, and he will heal our wounded spirits as time goes by.

Let's not forget that he is a high priest that can be touched with the feeling of our infirmities. One of the most stunning lines in the Bible, referring to the ability of Jesus to help us cope with grief, is to be found in Isaiah 53: "He was acquainted with grief." The Lord does not offer us empty condolences from a distance in the hour of our heartache. He has been there and he understands. Come to him in this hour. Don't try to solve it alone. That's what's wrong with our world; we have been trying to solve human problems with human solutions. It's time we start solving human problems with divine solutions. In John 14:1-3, he told his disciples not to have a troubled heart. He proposed a triple solution. First, have faith in God. He made the universe, and he is your Father, and he is in control. Second, have faith in me (Jesus); I went to a cross and died for your sins and solved the principal problem of the human race. Third, have faith in the future; in my Father's house are many mansions. We are on the way home. The trip gets somewhat rough at times, but soon we shall see him face to face.

Suffering and sorrow can often confuse us. Some of us have a tendency to become bitter when we ought to become better. We let the difficult hour separate us from the very source of help we need. "What a friend we have in Jesus, all our sins and griefs to bear." We can take our burden to the Lord and leave it there. He is a heart-mender. He knows how to heal broken hearts. The human mind, unaided by the ultimate purpose of the infinite Father, cannot decipher the deeper meaning of tears and trials. We need someone to give us insight. We need someone to walk with us and encourage our hearts in the desperate hour. So many in our day turn to chemicals like alcohol and drugs. And while doctors know the temporary value of chemicals when we are overwhelmed by sorrow and depressed by grief, they also know that a person who can solve his afflictions without recourse to the artificial aids is by far the wiser.

Job was stressing a solemn fact when he bemoaned that "man who is born of woman is of few days and full of trouble." Life is short, and just about the time we resolve one difficult situation, another one appears on the scene. We need the divine equipment to face this reality. Nothing is to be gained by cursing our fate or blaming God for stormy weather. That is the price we pay for being made in the image of God. We have a high capacity for suffering. We are sensitive, we can get hurt so easily because much of the trouble we confront in life is of our own making. We abuse our freedom—we sow to the wind and reap the whirlwind. We need to remember this and be willing to accept the consequences of our own deviations. We are also living in a world that groans under the curse of sin. Thorns and thistles, storms and tornados are the result of a world affected by the fall. These natural disasters can cause tremendous misery in our world.

Often our sorrow is caused by others. Our loved ones can be the biggest offenders. No one can hurt you like someone who is close, like a son or a daughter or a husband or a near relative. They, too, can abuse their freedom, and because we are near them, we feel the repercussions of their deviatory conduct. But no matter what the source of our despair may be, Jesus is there. The God who is smart enough to make the universe and sustain the orbital velocity of celestial bodies and feed the energetic bird and take care of the delicate flower, is able to care for his children. So come to him when you are sad, when life has dealt you a devastating blow, run to Jesus, run to Jesus. "He is a friend that sticketh closer than a brother."

III. Come to Jesus When You Are Bad

Not only come to him when you are glad and when you are sad, but come to him when you are bad. The infinite Savior knows that you are dust; he knows our frame, he knows our composition. He was tempted in all points, like as we, so he knows the force of the allurement of sin and the power of satanic onslaughts. He faced the devil often in his ministry; he is not ignorant of Satan's devices. But most of all, he confronted the power of iniquity on the cross; when he who knew no sin, became sin for us. So when you fail and are defeated, do not withdraw within yourself, do not rationalize your conduct by asserting that everyone is doing it, do not submerge your sins in the subconscious where they can do irreparable damage to your personality. Come to Jesus. He invites us in the text to do this.

So many accept the satanic suggestion that they cannot come to him and live the Christian life. The devil likes to make us think that the Christian life is not within the reach of the common man. But in the word of God, that objection is overruled. Jesus is able to save "from the uttermost to the guttermost." No combination of human corruptions can defeat the grace of God. The Lord is equal to our sins, and on the cross the total sin bill of the human race was expiated. Jesus paid it all. In the banquet of salvation, Jesus has picked up the tab; you cannot even leave the tip. The love of God has made provision for the vilest of sinners. Paul called himself the chief of sinners, but the grace of God could perform the miracle of mercy for this persecutor of the church who became one of the greatest trophies of redemption.

The dying thief was not reticent to come to Jesus. Here was a man who was dying at the hands of the government. Crucifixion was the technique employed by the Romans to execute offenders, analogous to our gas chamber or electric chair. Here was a man whom society said was not fit to live on the earth, and yet by one stroke of redeeming love, Jesus made him fit to live in heaven. If Christ can do it for one sinner, he can do it for all sinners. All the feeling he requires is to feel your need of him. Jesus cannot save us if we are self-sufficient. This poor man saw his need, he admitted that he was a sinner, he scolded the other thief for railing on Jesus. He said, "We are both in the same condemnation, we are sinners; this man Jesus is pure, He has done nothing amiss." So, in one stroke he affirmed his own corruption and accepted the divinity and perfection of Christ.

Look at the woman in John 4. She met Jesus at high noon at the well. In the beginning of the conversation, she did not want to confront the issue of her sinfulness and need. She tried to avoid her corruption by alluding to peripheral and marginal issues. She criticized Jesus for talking to her, for she was a Samaritan and "the Jews have no dealings with the Samaritans." She tried to discuss the race question. When that did not work, she tried to become historical. She reminded Jesus that father Jacob had dug the well and his cattle and children had drunk from it. When that didn't work, she tried to become theological and asked Jesus whether people should worship on the mountain in Samaria or in Jerusalem. She finally broke down and received the Lord, and running to town and telling everybody that she had met the Messiah, that she had received the Savior.

The Bible teaches that we are all sinners. We often call men good and bad, but the word of God has one expression for all of us, "Bad." In Romans 3:12, Paul said that "there is none that doeth good, no, not one." We are all bad, the only difference being that some of us are worse than others. We have all sinned and come short of the glory of God. Often when I talk to people about being saved, they inform me that they are just as good as the folks in the church where I am preaching. Why don't they tell the truth? They are just as bad as the folks in the church where I am preaching, and if one sinner needs to be in God's house looking for the solutions to his sins, every sinner should be there. But instead of saying they are as bad as others, they say they are as good as others. We are all bad, we are all sinners, and we need a divine intervention. We cannot save ourselves, nor can other human beings do it for us. Salvation is a miracle, and only Jesus can perform that miracle.

So Jesus is appealing to all sinners, "Come unto me." He is the balm in Gilead. He is God's remedy for our sins. When we become sick, we usually go to a doctor; when our watch breaks down, we take it to a watchmaker; when faucets leak, we call a plumber; when we want to remodel our house, we call a carpenter; when the car breaks down, we take it to a mechanic; when our soul needs saving, we must come to Jesus. He is the only One who can take imperfect human beings and make them sons and daughters of God. There is "none other name under heaven given among men, whereby we must be saved" (Acts 4:12). There is "one mediator between God and man, the man Christ Jesus" (1 Tim. 2:5). Come to him today!

3
The Biography of the Believer

And the disciples were called Christians first in Antioch.
(Acts 11:26)

Three times in the New Testament the followers of Jesus were called "Christians." The word *Christian* is used to describe the people who followed the Savior. Each time the word is used, it indicates an aspect of the life that the people of God exemplify. The first time it is used is the mention in the text above.

Some Bible students contend that this name was used in derision, like a certain religious group is called Campbellites or another group is called Russellites. But I think they were called Christians because of the way they lived. They were miniature Jesuses. They exemplified the love and forgiveness that characterized Christ. The second time it is used is in Acts 26:28, where Paul is conversing with King Agrippa concerning the sufferings and resurrection of Christ. Agrippa responds to Paul's appeal by saying, "Almost thou persuadest me to be a Christian." This second mention, I think, affirms the fact that believers have accepted the death and resurrection of Christ at the point of salvation. They have professed their belief that on the cross Jesus has expiated our sins, he has paid it all, and our transgressions have met their match at the cross. The third mention is in 1 Peter 4:16, where the apostle affirms that a Christian should not be ashamed if he has to suffer, and confronts that problem as a Christian. This indicates the fact that the believer's life is not going to be a bed of roses. Suffering is going to come from many sources as the people of God journey from the cradle to the grave. But the important fact is that we confront suffering in the spirit of Christ, as a Christian.

The life in Christ as a follower of the Savior is not going to be easy. But nothing good is easy. Jesus simplified salvation by his crucifixion so that every person can be saved who wants to be, and becoming a child of God is not difficult. But the Christian life is a cross. Not only did Jesus die on the cross for our sins, but we died with Jesus on that cross, and now we are to live the Christian life in the midst of a perverse generation.

It is not going to be easy. But if young people are willing to pay the price of laborious training to become great athletes, why shouldn't the believer be willing to bring his body under subjection in order to excel in the Christian race. If businessmen are willing to invest time and energy in becoming successful and earning money, why shouldn't the child of God be willing to pay the price to be rich in mercy and prosperous in the pursuit of spiritual treasures?

If a student is willing to discipline himself and study long hours and subtract himself from the pleasures of leisure in order to be an outstanding scholar, why shouldn't the Christian be willing to study to show himself approved, a workman that needs not to be ashamed, so he can rightly divide the word of truth.

But along with the disciplines of the Christian life, there are many delights. The child of God possesses an inner peace that the world does not know. It is the peace of Christ that makes it possible for us to assess the problems of life with composure and wisdom. So many believers go through life bemoaning the fact that they had to give up this and give up that in order to follow Christ. Why not concentrate upon the plethora of blessings that are ours in Christ Jesus? I have often heard preachers say that if they had not gone into the ministry, they would have been lawyers or doctors or college professors. I have to admit that if I had not been saved at the age of thirteen, I probably would have been a drunken bum on the streets of my hometown. Alcoholism was so prevalent in our Mexican culture that I would have drifted in that direction. The grace of God not only saved me from what I had been, but also from what I could have become.

The glorious joy of being a child of God forever fills me with constant awe. To this day, after forty-five years in the ministry, I marvel at the love of God. With Paul I have to say, "By the grace of God, I am what I am." If there were no heaven and no hell and no hereafter; if when men died, they died like animals and that was the end of them, I would still want to be the kind of person that a Christian is supposed to be. The present benefits that the Christian life provides would be worth the disciplines and the difficulties that are part and parcel of the life in Christ. So I am talking about the biography of the believer. Here it is in four chapters. The Book of God's children is described in these four ways. You will notice that with each point I use a preposition.

Chapter 1, Out of Christ

The Bible teaches that every human being needs to be saved. No one is born a child of God, even everyone is born a creature of God. But we have the glorious privilege of becoming God's children by faith in Jesus Christ. But in our natural state, we are sinners. The word for "sinner" in the Greek means "someone who is not perfect" and someone who has missed the mark. We are all imperfect; sometimes I wish we would use that word instead of the word sinner. When you call a man a sinner, often he thinks that you are calling him a thief or a murderer, but if you say to him that he is not perfect, that he has sinned one or more times, he would agree to that. We are all in that category—we are imperfect. "Al' we like sheep have gone astray; we have turned every one to his own way" (Isa. 53:6a). Paul tells us in the Roman epistle that "there is none that doeth good, no not one" (3:10). We are all bad, the only difference being that some of us are worse than others. We all came from the same mold, the only difference being that some of us are moldier than others!

David said that we begin to speak lies from birth. A woman heard me quote that and challenged it. She informed me that little babies cannot talk, and therefore they cannot lie. But I remember years ago when my first son was just a baby. We were in seminary, and one night that little creature began to cry. He let out a blood-curdling yell like he was dying. I said to my wife, "Get up and see what's wrong with *your* baby." She went to his little bed and picked him up, and he stopped crying. There were no tears in his eyes. He wasn't hurting but he wanted attention, and he acted like he was suffering; he sort of lied to get us to pick him up. So David was correct—our sinful nature can manifest itself very early.

The devil is busy trying to comfort sinners in their present condition and to upset Christians in order to keep them from being effective. Satan will whisper to the unsaved man, "You are all right; you are a good person; your moral life compares with those in the church; you don't need to be saved." Then that wicked accuser of the brethren tells the Christian, "You must not be saved. You do some horrible things, and you say dreadful things—therefore you must not be saved." So he tries to convince the unsaved man that he is saved, and he tries to convince the believer that he is lost. You can see that double work going on all of the time, and the devil has given false comfort to lost people and upset saved people by using this technique.

But every child of God knows that outside of Christ he was a lost person on the way to hell. And the believer knows that this was his condition before conversion. The Lord can never save people until they sense their need, until they realize that they are lost or imperfect. In Luke 18, Jesus relates a story about two men who came to the Temple to pray. One was a Pharisee, very moral and very proud. He strutted down the aisle and knelt at the altar, confessing other men's sins. He told the Lord that he was not a drunkard, not a murderer, not a thief. The publican, on the other hand, did not feel worthy to approach the altar. He knelt in the vestibule and cried, "God be merciful to me a sinner." The Scriptures state that the publican went home justified or saved. The Pharisee went home dignified. God cannot do business with people who are not willing to admit that they need a Savior. We are sinners, and our own efforts cannot make us acceptable in the sight of God.

A man can no more save himself than a flat tire can fix itself. A flat tire can be fixed, but someone else must do it, and sinners can be saved, but someone else must do it for them. The fact that you are not as bad as others does not score points with God.

No combination of human goodnesses can make us acceptable in the sight of a perfect God. You could resurrect the thousand best people that ever lived and take from each one his best and combine the thousand goodnesses into one individual. Wouldn't that be a terrific person? With all of that combined goodness, one might try to claim that person did not need to be saved. Yet, that individual, with all of that compounded character and goodness (and with his compounded badness, too), would still have to kneel at the foot of the cross and say, "God be merciful to me a sinner."

Let us not forget that we are sinners before we sin. We are not sinners because we sin. We sin because we are sinners. A dog is not a dog because he barks. He barks because he is a dog. A cat is not a cat because he meows. He meows because he is a cat. A cow is not a cow because she moos. She moos because she is a cow.

We are born this way; this is the teaching of the Word of God. Well, you might say, "But I would not kill or steal or do some other things." This may be true, but your sins are expressed differently. Listen, any sin that any sinner commits, every sinner could commit under the proper pressure. That is why James told us that if we offend the law in one point, we have broken it in every point. If you have it in you to break commandment number ten, which exhorts us not to covet, you have it in you to break number nine, number, eight, number seven and the rest of them—if the pressure and conditions were right. This sinful state is true of the entire human race. "There is none righteous, no not one." The Christian knows that he was a child of disobedience, even as others (Eph. 2:1-3).

Chapter 2, In Christ

The believer in his former condition was out of Christ, but the condition changes; the grace of God moves in by faith and he is put into Christ. And because we are in Christ, we are new creatures (2 Cor. 5:17). And because we are in Christ, "there is therefore now no condemnation" (Rom. 8:1). Multitudinous blessings accrue to us because we are now in Christ. In 1 Corinthians 12:13, Paul tells us that by the Holy Spirit we are all baptized into the body of Christ. This glorious blessing is the greatest thing that happens to any human being. More important than becoming famous is to be a member of the body of Christ. More important than becoming wealthy is to have a position in Christ. More important than becoming educated is to be in Christ. This is the loftiest achievement that can transpire on the level of human experience—and it is God's good work.

This wonderful experience is made possible by the love of God, the grace of God. So 1 John 3:1 tells us to behold the manner of love that God has bestowed upon us that now makes us the sons of God. What makes the love of God so significant to me is its omniscience. God knows everything. He knows the number of times I am going to fail him and sin against him from point birth to point death. He knows my future as well as my past, and he still invites me to accept the gift of forgiveness and become a member of his family. We do not know everything. If we knew everything about our friends, their past and future, what they think, how they feel, possibly we might not call them friends. Our ignorance, in a way, is a blessing. Our human loves are based on ignorance. If you knew that your best friend would double-cross you or hurt you in the future, you would not like him now. But you don't know, and that ignorance becomes the basis of your friendship. But God knows everything about us, and he still loves us. That is "amazing grace, how sweet the sound, that saved a wretch like me."

The believer has found out that there is only one way to be saved. The child of God does not trust his good works, his character, or his religious activities for salvation. A woman in Miami told me that salvation can be approached from different directions. She commented, "For example, one can come into Miami in different ways. One can come in by boat, by air, by car, or one can walk in. In like manner people can go to heaven in different ways." I replied, "There is only one thing wrong with your argument. Heaven is not Miami." The Bible is clear in telling us that there is only one way. We are not being dogmatic when we say this—this is the teaching of the Word of God. We are not being exclusive or chauvinistic when we affirm that men can be saved no other way—this is spiritual law. This is what God has said, and his word is irrevocable.

So the believer is in Christ. What a glorious privilege, what a wonderful blessing. Did you ever stop to realize that the Christian can be only in one of two places at a time? He is either *in* Christ or *with* Him. And this spells victory either way. A little dying woman who was being consoled in the hour of her departure said, "Don't feel sorry for me. I am not looking for the undertaker, I'm looking for the uppertaker." This spirit of victory and optimism should encourage every one of us, no matter what the circumstances may be. You may be facing financial reverses; you may have children who are breaking your heart by taking detours that contradict everything you have taught them. You may have a vacant chair at your house—a loved one has departed and left a gaping hole in your life. You might be sick and facing surgery, but you can rejoice in the fact that "to live is Christ, and to die is gain" (Phil. 1:21).

Jesus has put a rainbow in our heart by virtue of our relationship to him. This is a promise; that the storms of judgment and condemnation will not invade our personal world. To be in Christ means that he has saved us forever. At the point of salvation, Jesus redeems us for eternity. God does not save us on the "installment plan." Did you ever stop to realize that you are just as saved one minute after you accept Christ as you ever will be? I have been in the ministry forty-five years; I am no more saved now than I was one second after I received the Savior as a shoeshine boy on the streets of San Antonio. Had I died one minute after I was saved, I would have gone to heaven just as surely as I am going now! All of the preaching, all of the study, all of the traveling has not made me more fit for heaven than I was one second after I received Christ.

So the believer is in a privileged position. His blessings in Christ are multitudinous. The Scripture catalogs at least thirty-six wonderful things that happen to the person who is in Christ. I do not have space to mention all of them, but they are the joys that we have in being related to Christ. In Luke 12:32, Jesus combines symbols and multiplies metaphors in telling us the blessings we have as Christians. He says in this passage, "Fear not, little flock (here we are referred to as being sheep of his, and he is the shepherd), for it is your Father's pleasure [here we are referred to as sons to a father] to give you the kingdom" [here we are referred to as royal subjects and he is the king—Author's comments in brackets].

Chapter 3, For Christ

The believer is not only out of Christ before he is saved, he is in Christ at the point of salvation; but he is also for Christ from point salvation to point death, or point second coming of Christ, whichever takes place first. Now that we have trusted Jesus and reaped all of the beautiful blessings that are ours by faith in Him, now we are to use our abilities, our talents, our time and our personality to glorify him. In Ephesians 2:8-10, we are reminded that we are saved by grace through faith; and it is a gift of God, not something we have earned by our efforts. But now, he continues in the passage, we are saved to serve. We are created unto good works which God has appointed that we should walk in them. What a privilege, what a joy to work for Jesus. What a blessing to be able to share with others the grace of God. He has made us colaborers with him. We are to be part of the team that tries to preach the gospel to every creature; for God is "not willing that any should perish, but that all should come to repentance" (1 Pet. 3:9).

People in the church, members of the family of God, need to become aggressive. People will work for political parties, school activities, and charity drives, but they expect the church to survive with no one doing anything. The Lord never meant us to serve him by merely being spectators on Sunday morning and listening to a choir sing and hearing a sermon from an eloquent pulpiteer. We need to go and exert holy boldness; we must take the offensive. Jesus said that he was sending us into the world like sheep among wolves. Notice the reversal of role. Usually, the wolves attack the sheep, but in this case the sheep are to attack the wolves! And we have the equipment with which to win. The power of the Holy Spirit is on our side. The ministry of prayer is on our side. The sharp two-edged sword of the Word of God is on our side. The angelic host is on our side. The presence of Jesus has been promised to go with us "even unto the end of the world."

What's wrong in the church is that many of us are not willing to go. We want to let others do the work. We plead that we are not effective, that we are too timid, that we are too busy, that we do not have the personality, and add myriads of excuses that are not acceptable in the sight of God. In many organizations there is the complaint that there are "too many chiefs and not enough Indians." The reverse is true in the church. We have too many Indians and not enough chiefs! We do not want to assume responsibility. And yet we are willing to work for civic organizations, involve ourselves in the political arena, and participate in the activities of the school. Do not misunderstand me, these wonderful institutions deserve our energies and cooperation, but if you have time for them and no time for the church that Christ purchased with his blood, then you are putting second things first and being disloyal to your primary concern.

Possibly the greatest contribution that believers can make to the kingdom of God is to win others to Christ. The privilege of sharing our faith cannot be done by an unbeliever. And it could be done so easily and systematically if every one involved himself just a little. Do you know that if one Christian won one person to Christ this year (the date of this release), and those two won just one each the next year, and those four would win just one each the next year and on and on; in 33 years, the length of the life of Jesus, four billion people would be saved. Winning one person to Christ a year is not unreasonable service. And yet thousands of churches in this country go year after year without one convert. How it must break the heart of Christ to see hundreds of Christians doing nothing when the harvest is white, but the laborers, the workers, are few.

We are saved to work. According to the Bible, we are soldiers, not tourists; we are servants, not house guests. We sing "Standing on the Promises," but most of us are sitting on the premises. God wants us to produce fruit. Jesus told a parable where a father said to his boy, "Son, go work in my vineyard today." And there is work to be done, but as far as serving is concerned, many of God's people are dead at this point. They think they are serving because they are coming to church or giving (many of them are not even doing that).

When my brother, Homer, was a little boy, he was playing with a black friend in an empty lot. They found a snake; and the black boy had a little hatchet with him, and they chopped the snake in two. The two pieces of the snake kept jumping and wiggling, and the two boys, on their haunches, watched with interest. The black boy turned to my brother and commented, "Homer, the snake is dead and don't know it." And many Christians are dead, as far as serving is concerned, and they don't know it.

Chapter 4, With Christ

Not only is the believer *out* of Christ and then *in* Christ and then *for* Christ, but ultimately, he will be *with* Christ. The Bible teaches that the moment a Christian dies, he goes to heaven. His body does not go—that awaits the resurrection. But the soul or the personality goes to heaven immediately. Paul taught this in 2 Corinthians 5:8, where he informs us that to be absent from the body is to be present with the Lord. The King James Version says "present with the Lord." The Greek has it: "face to face with the Lord." Did you ever stop to realize that the first face you will see when you die is the face of Jesus? The first face your saved mother saw when she died was the face of Jesus. The first face your Christian father saw when he died was the face of Jesus. The first face your baby saw when he died was the face of Jesus.

When the dying thief turned to Jesus and said, "Remember me, when you come into your kingdom," Christ replied, "Today you will be with me in paradise." Today, not after the judgment; today, not after the resurrection; today, not after you live a long time and serve me—today I am taking you to heaven. The Lord told him, "You will be with me, with me in heaven, in paradise." So when Christians die they go to be with Jesus. The Savior repeated that truth in John 14:1-3 when he told his disciples that in his Father's house were many mansions, and he told them that he was going ahead to make reservations. For what purpose? "That where I am, there you may be also." We are going to be with him where there is no night, no sorrow, no tears, no funerals, and no farewells. We are going to be with him where there are no wars, no poverty, no crime, and no sickness. We are going to be with him where there is no night because Jesus will be the illumination of the city.

There are many figures used for heaven in the Bible. It calls heaven a garden; it calls heaven a hotel; it calls heaven a country; but one of the most intriguing descriptions of heaven is in Revelation 21, where heaven is called a city. It will be a perfect cube, this New Jerusalem, with twelve gates, three on each side. The streets are paved with gold, the walls made of jasper, and the gates constructed of pearl. The twelve foundations are beautiful stones. And we are going to live inside this city; it will be our home with Jesus. Earth is our home now, but scientifically we live on the outside of our home. We are stuck on the surface of the earth. People in the arctic regions live on top of the house, those of us who live in America live on the side of the house, and the people in Australia live on the bottom of the house, stuck to the bottom. But in the New Jerusalem we will live in the house, not on it like we live now upon the earth. No one lives on top of his house. Only Snoopy in the "Peanuts" comic strip lives outside of his house. In our new home, we are going to live on the inside of that beautiful residence; we will be there forever, and we will be with Jesus.

So to live is Christ, and to die is gain. Think of it, child of God—we are moving in that direction. Some of our loved ones have already arrived there, and we are on the way. So no matter what happens down here—the illnesses, the broken hearts, the funerals—thank God we are moving to "a land that is fairer than day, and by faith we can see it afar." If you are reading me, and you are without Christ, trust Him as your Savior. And though by nature you are outside of Him, for we are all born that way, the moment you accept him, and you will be in him forever; then you can be for him as you serve Him, and someday you will be with him in that fair land!

4
Wait on the Lord

But they that wait upon the Lord shall renew their strength; they shall mount up with wings as eagles; they shall run, and not be weary; and they shall walk, and not faint. (Isaiah 40:31)

The Jews were in Babylon, in exile, far from their homeland and discouraged and depressed. They longed for the good old days; they pined for the Temple; they longed for their life-style. Here they were in the midst of strangers. They have hung their harps on the willow; they have lost their song. They were filled with fear, and they wondered when and how they were going to get home.

A day seemed like a thousand years, and the moments and the hours passed by so slowly. They couldn't find comfort in their own reasonings or among their fellow countrymen. They knew that they had sinned, or else they wouldn't have been in that pagan land. They rebelled against God's laws, and now the divine hand of chastisement had fallen upon them. They wept by day, and they had nightmares when they should have been sleeping. They were reaping what they had sown, but they didn't like the harvest of their own making!

The prophet Isaiah stepped into the picture and tried to inject a note of comfort into the sad song that they were singing. Prophets usually condemn and exhort the people for their sins and their lethargy; Isaiah tried to lay a healing hand upon their broken spirits. But he did not offer them a mythical assurance. The comfort that he offered was based upon the fact that their sins had been confessed and forgiven. So many in our day want comfort without confession; they want peace of mind without pardon of soul. So in verse 1 of Isaiah the prophet based comfort upon the forgiveness of iniquity. He let them know that the path from Babylon to Jerusalem was a wilderness, but he assured them that God was building a road back to their land (verses 3-5). Sin always separates God's people from the place He has designed for them.

But the prophet had to take his eyes off of humanity in order to find a solution to the problem. In verses 6-8, he wailed about the brevity of life. Man is like grass and soon withers; man is like a flower and soon fades. We cannot find the answer to the ills of man by looking within; we must look above to the One whose power and love never dim or die; they never fade or fail. There is change and decay in everything we see, but God, who changes not, can usher us out of the bondage provoked by our corruption and sin. The rest of the chapter affirms the power and love of God as the foundation for the hope of the chosen people. So our hope is in God, not in ourselves. All of our sorrows, all of our problems, all of our tears can find their resolution in the person of God. So many of us spend our days applying human solutions to human situations. We must learn how to wait on the Lord.

Isaiah pictures God as being strong like a warrior (verse 10) and gentle like a shepherd (verse 11). These two qualities were important at that time to the captive people. To them it would prove that God was superior to the pagan deities of the Babylonians if he could release them from the bondage of captivity and wrest them from the grip of these foreign gods. So God is pictured as a strong person who carries his might in his arm. But then he is also symbolized as a shepherd. The people needed someone tender to heal their wounded spirits. God's omnipotence and love are essential qualities that every one of us needs. We are living in a world where we wrestle not against flesh and blood; we are fighting principalities and powers and wickedness in high places, the hosts of hell. We need the strong name of the Trinity to rescue us and do for us what we cannot do for ourselves. But at the same time, we need a shepherd who will apply kindness and tenderness to our destitute situation. "All we like sheep have gone astray." We need someone to guide us and to love us and to comfort us as we journey between the cradle and the grave.

So Isaiah concludes the chapter by urging the people to wait on the Lord. They had been so embittered by the captivity that they thought the Lord had abandoned them (verse 27), but this was not so. You may think, my friend, that amid your heartache and defeat that God has forgotten you. But the prophet reminded them, in verse 28, that God is in control, that in the shadows, God is standing and watching over his own. God is not in a hurry, but he is never late. Our task is to learn how to wait on him. The word "wait" in the Hebrew encourages us to wait with eagerness; God is going to do something about the situation. We try to syncopate the Lord. We try to make him fit our herky-jerky schedule. But he has his own timetable and his own way. If we learn to wait on him, he will reward us with the promises in our text. He will give us power over temptation; he shall renew our strength. He will give us power over depression; we shall mount up with wings as eagles. He will give us power over emergencies; we shall run and not be weary. He will give us power over monotony; we shall walk and not faint.

I. Power over Temptation

The prophet Isaiah informs us that the Lord will give us power over temptation. He shall renew our strength. Westermann says that he is talking here about a certain kind of strength—a moral, an inner strength. He is not talking about physical strength. And the people of Isaiah's day needed this kind of reinforcement. In the midst of their captivity, they had to fight the temptation to become bitter and the many sins that accompany a discouraged spirit. We are living in a dirty world. The allurements of the present age are very enchanting. The world, the flesh, and the devil are still in operation. The battle against evil within and without never ceases. But we are not alone. God has promised to give us a strength that will match the temptations that surround us. The word "renew" means that he will keep on doing it. The attacks of this present world are unrelenting and we cannot relax our vigil. God has promised to keep on giving us strength, which means that we need a daily infusion of power because the forces of sin never give up.

Let us not forget that at the point of our salvation the Lord did not eliminate the old sin nature which we acquired from Adam. Many Christians have the idea that when they became converted, the attacks of Satan will diminish, and the flesh will reduce its impact against the spirit. Not so. The battle may intensify. When Jesus was baptized and began his public ministry, the devil escorted him into a high mountain, and we are all familiar with the triple temptation that Satan used to try to divert the mission of the Master at its very inception. After the dove came the devil; after the baptism came the battle; after the voice from heaven came the roar from hell.

So we have an old sin nature that is not erased at the point of salvation. The Lord knows this, and he has made provision for victory by the presence and power of the Holy Spirit. That is why in the Lord's Prayer we are instructed to say, "Forgive us our sins." Some of the Greek commentators contend that the word "this day" in the preceding verse, "give us this day our daily bread," should jump over to the next verse, and it should read, "and forgive us this day our sins." So the confession of sin is as essential to the well-being of our spiritual lives as the ingestion of nutrition is important to our physical lives. And even as we eat daily, we need to confess our sins *daily*. And through the power of confession, we can win the victory over temptation. The Holy Spirit begins to widen the gap between confession and the recommission of sin, and in this way we grow in grace. There are no short cuts to sanctification or Christian growth.

Paul told us in 1 Corinthians 10:13 that we would be tempted. But with every temptation, God has made a way for our escape. We cannot do it alone. We cannot win the victory in the energy of the flesh. So many believers are trying to resolve the problem of sin and failure through their efforts. The road of life is littered with failures because Christians were not willing to tap the resources God has made available through his grace. His grace is sufficient, and his strength is made perfect in weakness. We must learn how to lean on the everlasting arms. There is no need for defeat and failure when God has made his strength available to us. To be sure, the devil is strong and clever, the flesh is enticing and the world is alluring, "but greater is he that is in you, than he that is in the world" (1 John 4:4).

When Simon Peter was faltering, the Lord informed him that Satan was trying to sift him like wheat, but Christ reassured the wobbling disciple that he was praying for him that Peter's strength would not fail. The Lord is praying for us, and we need to know that he who died on the cross was tempted in all points, like as we, and won the victory of the resurrection. One day he is coming back. He is on our side, and he can sympathize with our situation. He faced heartaches, physical pain, the onslaughts of Satan, the heartache of departed loved ones, the treachery of trusted friends. Armed with all that experience, and knowing the nature of man, Christ is sufficient, and he wants to help us to win the victory and to be "more than conquerors through him that loved us" (Rom. 8:37*b*).

In Ezekiel 44 it is reported that Aaron and the priests had to wear linen into the holy place; they could not wear wool. In other words, God did not want a priest who sweats. And many of us are trying to win the victory by struggles and grunts when we could rely upon the power of the Spirit. I see so much huffing and puffing in Christian living today. And this confuses the unsaved man. He is having a struggle in his world, and he does not want to swap one set of struggles for another. We should demonstrate to the world the calmness and the relaxed attitude that Christ can give as we try to win the victory in the battle of life.

II. Power over Depression

Not only will he give us power over temptation, but he will give us power over depression. The text says that "we shall mount up with wings as eagles." There are many ups and downs in the life we live, but God will give us the victory over the downs, if we learn how to wait upon him. Depressions are common in our day, and they can happen to the best of us. The competitive culture in which we live, the pressure caused by others in the home and out of it, the feeling of insecurity that abounds everywhere, and many other factors can cause us to feel low and blue. Do not be surprised if this happens to you. So many of us are baffled by these basement emotions, and we must learn how to deal with them effectively. You cannot be a fulfilled person in the game of life if you are morose and dejected all of the time. From the pit of gloom and darkness, God can give us wings so we can emerge from these miserable moods that want to imprison our spirits.

In a grand fashion God has made provision for our escape. The eagle has always been a symbol of strength and greatness, and the Word of God uses this majestic bird to represent the way we can triumph over our despair. The child of God does not have to resort to chemical solutions in order to score over low moods. I know that in extreme cases people have to lean upon medication for a while. But in the regular grind of everyday living, provision has been made by the grace of God so we can live effectively. And I am convinced that people get on drugs or alcohol when they have not learned how to deal with their moods on a day-by-day basis. They are defeated by minor irritations, and then these minute afflictions compound themselves until they produce situations that are difficult to manage.

We must always remember that we have a friend in Jesus and that he is sympathetic with our moods. You recall that John the Baptist became depressed. One day he sent a delegation to the Master to inquire about His mission. This great prophet was confused for he had been languishing in jail and friends had been negligent in his hour of need. Jesus was performing works of mercy when John thought that He should be executing works of judgment. In this abysmal mood he asked Christ if he were the true Messiah, or should he look for someone else.

I am sure the crowd was shocked at this question coming from a man like John. But here, again, was a case in point; it can happen to the best of us. But did Jesus condemn him? No, he sought to comfort him with a compliment. Notice how tender Jesus was with this doleful disciple. He told the crowd that of all men born of women, there was none greater than John the Baptist. That was a terrific statement. Do you realize that this included Moses, Jeremiah, Abraham, and David? The Savior said that John was in the class of those ancient heroes (Matt. 11:11). And he told the delegation sent by John that the blind were seeing, the lame were walking, and the poor had the gospel preached to them.

Elijah, that stately old prophet of the Old Testament, became depressed. After the stunning victory on Mount Carmel, he went into a slump. He ran from Jezebel who had vowed that she would kill him, and under a juniper tree he begged God to let him die (1 Kings 19:4). But God intervened and ministered to the physical needs of the fatigued prophet. Often, depressions are physical disorders. Our bodies have a way of disturbing our emotional pattern. It is easy for the endocrine system to lose its balance and provoke bizarre moods within us. But the Lord did not condemn Elijah for those emotional lows, but rather God sought to help him, and He will do it for us.

We are a peculiar generation. Our scientific progress is amazing, and yet simple problems elude our solutions. We are smart enough to walk on the moon, but not safe enough to walk in the park. We have more affluence, more wealth, more material possessions than any other generation, and yet we are low in spirit with our moods dragging. We have more labor-saving devices than ever before, and yet we are the most tired people of all time. We ought to be the most rested and the most joyful, but our prosperity and mobility have not brought us the inner victory of a joyful spirit. That is why God is so indispensable. Without him we are a bundle of contradictions. We need his grace to untangle our aberrant moods and unscramble our confused emotions. We need to wait on the Lord. We have tried human solutions, and the pollution of our day deepens. Our depressed spirits reflect the inability of pleasures and material prosperity to present the peace that passes understanding and misunderstanding.

Wait on the Lord! There is the answer to our depressions. So many of us are not theoretical atheists—we are practical atheists. I heard of a poll which stated that only 85 percent of the Methodists believe in God, 92 percent of Presbyterians believe in God, and the Baptists fared a little better—95 percent of them believe in God. But had the poll included demons, they would have scored 100 percent, because there is no atheism among demons; the demons believe in God and tremble (Jas. 2:19). Only human beings with ungrateful hearts are guilty of atheism. And we need God more than any other creature on God's earth. We are made in the image of God, and we are more sensitive and have more potential than the beasts of the field or the birds of the air or the fish in the water.

III. Power over Emergencies

Not only will waiting on the Lord furnish power over temptations and power over depression, but God has promised power over emergencies—"they shall run and not be weary." And the day is coming when we are going to run. The desperate hour will come upon us sooner or later. And while life is made up mostly of dull and routine experiences, we do not live too long before the dreadful hour of heartaches will descend upon us. For such a time, we are going to need the presence and the power of God. We are no match for these difficult times. We need help from above and beyond. And God has promised to accompany us in "the valley of the shadow of death." The Jews were facing an emergency situation in Babylon. Other problems they had were nothing in comparison to the tragedy of being transported to a heathen land and forced to live in an environment that contradicted every holy aspiration they had known in Jerusalem.

But God can take every Calvary and turn it into an Easter Sunday. Difficult hours are the raw material out of which we can weave a garment of praise for the glory of God. You will never have a greater opportunity to glorify the Lord than when darkness invades your experience, and the storm clouds form across the sky of your life. God will reveal himself to you unforgettably during the sadness and grief that accompany drastic emergencies. You will learn more about God's power, patience, and proximity when your heart has been broken than when you study books or try to learn lessons from the afflictions of others.

And do not forget that none of us will be exempt from the tornados of life. The fact that you are a faithful Christian or a concerned human being, trying to do your best to live right and help others, will not avert the fact that storms will come to each and all. In the famous Sermon on the Mount, Jesus related a story about two houses, one built on the rock, the other built on the sand. But the rains descended, and the storms came, and the winds blew on the house built upon the rock just as they came upon the house built on the sand (Matt. 7:24-28).

The apostle Paul is a case in point. His life was filled with storms. If goodness, devotion, and heroism should exempt a person from dark hours, the apostle Paul would have qualified. And yet, he, who gave himself with unflagging devotion to the cause of Christ, had to face emergency situations almost daily. In 2 Corinthians 11:24 and following, he tells about a few of these problems that he had to confront. The Jews scourged him at least five times; he was beaten with rods three times; he was stoned at Lystra and left for dead; he suffered shipwreck on several occasions, and on one of them he was in the water for twenty-four hours. He was always on the road, and robbers were abundant in that day, operating without restraint. The people to whom he ministered often misunderstood him and became his enemies.

His own people to whom he ministered were often against him. People who disagreed with him on doctrinal matters made his life unbearable. He was not physically well and suffered constant pain. There were times when he was hungry, and other times he could not get water to quench his thirst. He faced bad weather; often he did not have clothing to protect him against the cold. And yet he tells us that we can do all things through Christ which strengthens us (Phil. 4:19); and he also reminds us that everything that happens to us down here is nothing in comparison to the glory that shall be ours in the sweet bye and bye (Rom. 8:18).

We cannot decipher the meaning of extreme suffering with our minds. When you look up to heaven in the midst of a difficult encounter, and you ask God why this or that had to happen, you are not looking for an answer. You are looking for an argument, and God is not going to argue with you or me. We are not smart enough to argue with the Lord. He knows some things about life and about us that we do not know. Only in retrospect, as we look back, are we going to see the meaning to many things that baffled us when we were going through them. We have a poor perspective of the present. We do not know how to read the true meaning of what is happening now. That is why we must learn how to take our burden to the Lord and leave it there. But so many people become bitter when the storms come instead of becoming better. Many of us get angry with God because we do not understand why the baby died or the sickness came. But he has promised special strength to those who learn how to trust in him. Jesus encouraged us to have faith in God. Without faith, it is impossible to please him (Heb. 11:6).

IV. Power over Monotony

Not only will he give us power over temptation and power over depression and power over emergencies, but he will give us power over monotony—"we shall walk and not faint." Life is composed of the trite and inconsequential. The storms and the tornados come and go, and they come in different stages of our life. But the humdrum and the prosaic are with us always. The termites, not the tornados, are the basic problem of human existence. We must learn how to handle the details and peccadillos of everyday living. An inability to do this can provoke some grave problems. I have seen many people stand firm in the midst of trying hours and then collapse in the dull routine of life. Many of us think that the Lord is there only when the big problems arise, but he is also concerned in the little things. He is a God of the infinite and also a God of the infinitesimal. He is a God of the macroscopic and also a God of the microscopic. The very hairs on our heads are numbered, and when a sparrow dies, an insignificant creature, God attends his funeral.

Many people live lives that lack luster, and perhaps they think that they do not count for much in the sight of God. But I believe that God is glorified by individuals who are able to walk and not faint. We are told in John 10:41 that John did no miracle. Here was a man who was faithful in the discharge of everyday duties. Life was not one big excitement for him. Yet Peter and Paul and other disciples and apostles lived exciting lives. But here was a man who was faithful in little things. He did not do anything spectacular, but he was constant in his life and devotion to the Lord. These kinds of people compose the bulk of the kingdom of God. And I think there is an art in being able to live in the midst of dullness and anonymity, and God will reward people who can "fill the unforgiving minute with sixty seconds worth of work well done," as Kipling put it.

So do not think, my friend, that you are not accomplishing much simply because your service does not make the headlines or because you are not the quarterback on God's team. God glories in the patient labor of those who do their best in the quiet place. And he will not ignore this kind of service. It was Jesus who complimented the small gift of the widow, while others were donating rich contributions into the coffers of the Temple. So the Lord has promised to reward even a cup of cold water that is given in his name (Matt. 10:42). Have you won the victory in this area? If you wait on the Lord, he has promised to strengthen you not only for the difficult hour but also for the times that are monotonous and sluggish.

The Bible teaches that the kingdom of God is within us. So if the kingdom is within us, then the King is also there. And where the King is, life is not commonplace. We tend to think that the Lord is only with us in emergencies, but he is also there when we are walking faithfully in our daily routines. I know that we often feel discouraged when big things are not happening in our lives, and we look at others who are serving in a colorful fashion and getting attention. We are like the little boy who was sitting on the bank with the pole in his hand and the hook in the water, but nothing was happening. He had been sitting there for hours, but no success—not even a nibble. An old man passed by and said, "Son, what are you doing? Are you fishing?" The little boy replied glumly, "I'm not fishing. I'm just drowning worms." And many of us feel that way, but the Lord does not look at it like that. He rejoices in our consistency, and his joy should make our work worthwhile.

When God made the universe in six days, the Bible tells us that he rested on the seventh day. He did not rest because he was tired. He rested because he was finished. Everything he does is perfect, and some of the greatest realities are little things. The microscopic world is a beautiful one. Things are not to be despised because they are small. The big organs in the body function because little cells and vessels are being faithful in the discharge of their duty. In 1 Corinthians, Paul is talking about the functions of large organs like eyes and ears and hands and feet. But he reminds us that the small and uncomely parts of the body are very important and should not be despised (1 Cor. 12:23). So God glorifies the small, and nothing is insignificant to him.

God is not going to make us fit to live in heaven and then make us unfit to live on the earth. He knows our composition; he knows that we are dust; he knows that we are going to have slow hours and dull seasons, and he has made provision for giving us the inner strength to cope with those times. So many of us want to live lives like the display of fireworks instead of the constant shining of the stars. A fireworks show attracts attention for a few minutes and outdazzles the stars in the heavens, but when the show is over, the heavenly bodies continue their faithful witness in the blue. And the Lord wants us to be faithful, and he will give us grace to walk and not faint if we are willing to wait upon him and trust his power and not rely on our own weaknesses.

5
We'll Work Till Jesus Comes

And Samuel said unto Jesse, Are here all thy children? And he said, There remaineth yet the youngest, and behold, he keepeth the sheep. And Samuel said unto Jesse, Send and fetch him: for we will not sit down till he come hither. (1 Samuel 16:11)

God had rejected Saul as the king of the chosen people. He was backslidden and had disobeyed the commands of God and had become a defective ruler. The Lord came to Samuel in this chapter and commanded him to go to the house of Jesse where he would find the future ruler of the people. Samuel was afraid *what if Saul finds out.* And he expressed his fear of the king to the Lord. Saul had fits of temper that would drive him to murder, and Samuel feared for his life. The Lord informed his prophet that he had nothing to fear. He instructed him to go to Bethlehem, where David was residing, and to carry a sacrificial animal as though he were going to make an offering to the Lord in the city.

Samuel obeyed, and, when he arrived in the city, the elders questioned him as to why he was there. The prophet assured them that he was there on a mission of peace and worship. He invited the elders and the house of Jesse to attend this act of celebration to the Lord. After the sacrifice, Samuel began to look at the sons of Jesse to determine the will of the Lord with reference to the next king of Israel. The old prophet was impressed with Eliab. He was tall and handsome, and Samuel was convinced that this was God's choice. But not so. God reprimanded his messenger for judging spiritual worth on the basis of external features. Thus, we have the famous statement in verse 7 that man looks on the outward appearance, but God looketh in the heart. God looks at inner beauty; often we judge by the tip of the iceberg, by what we see on the outside. God told Samuel that tall, dark, and handsome Eliab was not his choice.

So the prophet insisted that Jesse show him the rest of the boys. So Abinadab and Shammah and all of the other sons passed before Samuel, but the Lord approved none of those. In despair, Samuel said to Jesse, "Have you shown me all of them?" Jesse confessed that he did not bring in one of the boys. He was young, and he was taking care of the sheep. At that point, God's messenger expressed the words of our text. He said to Jesse, "I do not want to miss a single one. I do not care if he is young, and you have given him the insignificant task of tending the sheep. Run and get him, for we will not sit down till he comes."

When David walked in, garbed in the attire of a shepherd, but beautiful without and within, God said to Samuel, "There is my man; get the oil and anoint him king of Israel." The Spirit of the Lord came upon David. God had equipped him for the task of ruling the chosen people. And we know the rest of the story. I want to show that David is a type of Christ. David was a shepherd, and so is Christ. David became king, and so will Christ become king when he returns the second time. What shall we do? The words of our text furnish the answer. We will not sit down till He comes.

I. Jesus as Shepherd

David was a shepherd, and so is Jesus Christ. Even in the Old Testament, David said, "The Lord is my shepherd." In our present dispensation Jesus is the shepherd, and we are members of his flock. You remember that in Matthew 16 he asked his disciples, "Whom do men say that I am?" They replied that some said he was Jeremiah, others said that he was Elijah, others said that he was John the Baptist, and others said he was some other prophet, maybe Moses. Though other men had various names and opinions about him, Jesus called himself a shepherd. In John 10:11 he said, "I am the good shepherd; the good shepherd giveth his life for the sheep." And in that verse he described his life and death. When he said he was good, this indicated his perfect life and incarnation. When he said that he gave his life for the sheep, he was giving us a glimpse of his atoning death.

Jesus was a living shepherd. He existed before eternity. He was with the Father at creation. He made repeated visits to the earth in the Old Testament. I am convinced that it was Jesus who came to the Garden of Eden and asked, "Adam, where art thou?" And throughout the Old Testament he made many appearances before he was incarnated in the manger. In John 8:58 he told the Pharisees that "before Abraham was, I AM." He did not say that "before Abraham was, I was." He is not saying that he existed before Abraham. He was saying that he had always existed. He is the eternal I AM. John 1:3 states, "All things were made by him, and without him was not anything made that was made."

This Living Shepherd entered the stream of human history at the incarnation when the "word was made flesh and dwelt among us." He was bone of our bone and flesh of our flesh—and yet without sin. He walked among men and experienced the dilemmas and problems of human existence. He became involved in our trials and temptations. No one can say that He is not adequate, that He cannot sympathize, that He does not care. He can mend our broken hearts; he can wipe clouds from human skies; he can help us when we stumble; he can comfort us when loved ones say good-bye; he can console us when the home crumbles; he can inspire us when we are depressed; he can calm us when anxieties overwhelm our spirits.

This Living Shepherd died and remained in the grave for three days. But he arose and lives to help us and to walk with us in the valley of the shadow of death. Revelation 1:18 affirms that he was alive and then death came; but he conquered the grave, and he is alive forevermore. Had he remained in the grave, we would still be in our sins, our faith would have no meaning, our preaching would be in vain, and our loved ones who have died would have vanished forever—and we would be of all men most miserable. This is the teaching of 1 Corinthians 15:16-19.

He is not only a Living Shepherd, but he is a Loving Shepherd. The love of Jesus for his sheep is a mystery. One thing that astounds me about the love of our Savior is its omniscience. He knows everything about us, and he still loves us. He knows the past. We have a tendency to forget the past, especially the things that we do not like about ourselves. The psychologists tell us that we repress, or stow away in the subconscious, the acts and attitudes that we dislike about ourselves. But Jesus knows the content of the subconscious, and he still loves us. Not only that, he knows the future. The future is unknown to us, but he is conversant with every sin, every failure, every evil thought, and every sinful act that we are going to commit from point now until point death, and he still loves us.

Human loves are built on ignorance. We love others because we do not know too much about them, and they do not know too much about us. If you knew what your best friend thinks about you, you might not like him, and if he knew what you have thought and said about him, he might not like you. But Jesus knows the past and the future, and, knowing all of that, he still opens wide his arms and invites us to come to him and be saved.

His love is reliable. You can trust someone who loves you that much. If someone came to you and said, "I love you so much I would die for you," you would say, "There's a real friend. If I ever have troubles, I am going to him." Friend, Jesus loves you that much. He died for you and proved his love by that atoning sacrifice. You can trust him with your trials and your troubles. You can trust him with your sins and your sorrows. You can trust him with your yesterdays and your tomorrows, and love like that deserves your best response, your time, your personality, your abilities, your all.

Not only is he a Living Shepherd and a Loving Shepherd, but he is a Life-giving Shepherd. John 10:27-30 teaches this touching truth. Jesus said that his sheep would hear his voice and follow him. Now these are not conditions; he did not say that *if* they heard his voice, and *if* they followed him, he would give them eternal life. These are characteristics, not conditions. And he promised them a beautiful life; he said that he would give them eternal life. Note that it is a gift, not a loan. When someone lends you something, you have to return it. It is not yours. This life is a gift; you do not work for it, you do not earn it. It is the gift of Christ to you. And do not forget that it is eternal. That means it never ends. Nothing can terminate it—your sins cannot end it, your problems in life cannot end it, your failures cannot end it, it is eternal. If you could lose it in three months, it would not be eternal; if you could lose it in a year, it would not be eternal; if you could lose it the next time you commit a sin, it would not be eternal.

A person cannot be unsaved after he has been saved any more than he can be unborn after he has been born. This is the way God chose to do it. But there are many who believe that sin is stronger than grace. If any of my sins can undo what Jesus did for me on the cross, then my sins are stronger than the crucifixion. The Bible does not teach that. If I disobey him and disappoint him after I have been saved, he can take a switch and come after me, but he will not send me to hell.

And for fear that someone would not understand the positive statement, the Lord said it again in a negative way, "And they shall never perish." It is like writing a check. When you write a check, you indicate the amount twice. You write, "Pay to the order of John Doe," and then you place the amount in numbers on the right-hand side, and then you drop down to the next line, and in long hand you write the amount again, and then you sign it. So Jesus made a check payable to "Whosoever will," and on the right-hand side he wrote "eternal life," and then he dropped down on the next line and said it again: "And they shall never perish, signed, Jesus Christ." And friend, that is a good check—it will never bounce.

II. Jesus Becomes King

Even as David the shepherd became a king, even so Jesus, our Shepherd, will become King when he comes the second time. The Bible teaches that he is not sitting on his Father's throne. He is at the right hand of God the Father making intercession for us, and he has been doing that for the last 2,000 years. I am grateful for the prayers of friends and loved ones. I am thankful for the prayers of my mother for my ministry. I think if God is partial to anyone, he is partial to the prayers of mothers. So mothers, pray for your children, pray for our world. But most of all, I am grateful for the prayers of Jesus. It is wonderful to know that he is interceding for me at the right hand of the Father.

But Matthew 25:31 teaches that when Christ comes the second time, then shall he sit upon the throne of his glory. He who came the first time to redeem is coming the second time to reign. He who came as a Savior is coming again as a Sovereign. The King is coming, as the popular song states it. In fact, the Bible declares that he will be King of kings and Lord of lords. Earthly kingdoms will rise and fall, nations have come and gone, mighty rulers have exerted their power and then crumbled into dust, but Jesus is coming again as King, and he shall rule forever.

There are many in our day who are not looking for him. The intellectual and modern theologians have discarded the concept that Christ will come again. But the Word of God reminds us repeatedly that he who came the first time will return. There are 7,957 verses in the New Testament, and 323 of them promise that Christ will come a second time. So to the average of one verse in every twenty-five, the New Testament reveals this tremendous truth. The Holy Spirit inserted frequent reminders so the church would never forget her magnificent tomorrow. Second Peter 3:4 states that the scoffers will affirm continuity and deny the visible return of our Lord, yet the recurring theme of the New Testament is the glorious appearing of our great God and Savior, our Lord Jesus Christ.

In Titus 2:11-13 Paul contends that the grace of God that brings salvation has appeared to all men. He encourages us to live righteously and godly in this present evil world. He motivates us by exhorting us to look for the blessed hope. The word "blessed" in the Greek is the word for happy. In other words, the return of our King will be a happy event. Often I meet people who tell me they do not like to discuss the end of time. It terrifies them to think that this present world system will end. They think that the coming of Christ will bring more sorrow and despair, and there is enough of that already in our time. But they are mistaken; they have not learned that the coming of Jesus will bring happiness. When the event of his return is consummated, all of the things which make for unhappiness in our world will vanish. When Jesus comes again, man will study war no more. All the war colleges will close when Jesus returns. West Point will shut its doors when Jesus comes again. The Air Force Academy will close its doors when Jesus comes again and all of the military schools will go out of business when Jesus comes again.

Poverty and destitution will be no more when Jesus comes again. Our hearts are heavy when we hear that children are starving and that many people in our world go to bed hungry. We have been blessed in this country; we have food in abundance, but there are many nations where this is not so. But when Christ returns this condition will no longer prevail. No wonder it will be a happy event. Death will be no more when Jesus comes again. Death will be swallowed up in victory. There are no good-byes in heaven. Our hearts are broken when loved ones have to leave. Death knocks on every door sooner or later. "It is appointed unto man once to die," and "man who is born of woman is of few days and full of trouble." But one of these days, death will come no more. No more funeral corteges; no more weeping for loved ones that are gone. Never again will the preacher say, "Ashes to ashes and dust to dust." The victory is coming when the King returns. No wonder Paul called it a "happy hope."

In 1 Thessalonians 4:16, the great apostle reminded us of this great and glorious truth. Jesus shall descend from heaven "with a shout, the voice of the archangel, and the trump of God." Some Bible students contend that the shout is for the Christians who have died in the Lord and shall be resurrected and their bodies immortalized. The voice of the archangel is for the Jew; he will be cognizant of the Lord's coming to the world, and the trumpet of God will be for the living Christians who shall never die and whose bodies shall be translated and caught up in the clouds to meet the Lord in the air, never again to be separated from him. The reference to clouds is a unique one. Paul is not giving us a weather report, but he is describing a traffic jam. The clouds refer to multitudes who will go up to meet Jesus. The word is used in the same sense in Hebrews 12:1 where the writer talks about being compassed about with "so great a cloud of witnesses."

I am so glad that our King is coming. Man does not have the solution to human pollution. Our sociology and technology are not enough; we need help from above. Even as man could not save himself individually, and Christ came the first time and said, "I will do it for you," so man cannot save himself internationally, and Christ again says, "I will come again and do it for you." When he came the first time, that was Operation Grace; when he comes the next time, that will be Operation Glory.

The screaming headlines announcing the rattling of sabers and the constant preparation for armed conflict make it imperative that Jesus, our King, must return. The sky of human history is filled with ominous and foreboding clouds, and it looks like the storms of war and bloodshed are about to break. Troubles in the Middle East, troubles in Africa, troubles in South American countries all indicate that soon the world will be engulfed by the hurricane of conflict and carnage. The military build-up in China, in Russia, in Cuba are all foreboding signs that things are not well among nations. Last year, the nations spent almost a trillion dollars preparing for war. They tell us that in Europe alone there are at least 3,000 nuclear missiles facing each other, ready to be detonated at a moment's notice. The next war will not last long. Within the span of an hour, millions will die and cities will be demolished. Even so, come, King Jesus.

The coming of Jesus is the only hope for this world. Some intellectuals think that this doctrine is a form of escapism. They have misnamed it; it is the only hope of the church, and the only solution to human history. This does not mean that we are to fold our hands and do nothing since Jesus is coming again. This great hope and truth should motivate us to do everything we can to correct our social structure, but at the same time to realize the limitations of our culture. If you read history, you will discover that the people who did the most for this present world were the ones who lived in the hope of the next world. The modern mood of disclaiming the reality of the next world has made us ineffective in this one. C. S. Lewis, the great Oxford professor, said, "Aim at Heaven, and you get earth thrown in; aim at earth, and you will get neither."

III. What Shall We Do?

Jesus, our Shepherd, will come as our King. What shall we do? The answer is in the text; we will not sit down till he comes. We'll work till Jesus comes. Every believer, looking for the soon return of Christ, should get busy with the spiritual tasks that lie before him and around him. We are not to go to a hill somewhere and abandon the common tasks and wait for his return. The way to make the second coming of our King relevant and scriptural is to get busy winning people to Christ and trying to heal this wounded society that rocks and reels in the throes of its own confusion and despair. Jesus never glorified laziness and indolence. He "went about doing good." His was a life of action and involvement, and there is no conflict between believing in a soon-coming Lord and plunging our talents, personalities, and time in an attempt to resolve the heartaches of our day.

Jesus said, "Let him that is the greatest among you be the servant of all." We are to work, and there is so much to do. Jesus did not judge men by their income. He judged them by their outgo. He never judged a man by how many servants he had, but by how many people he served. When his disciples would reduce eschatology to discussion in Acts 1:5, he reminded them that there was work to do. He told them to be his witnesses in Jerusalem and Samaria and Judea and to the uttermost parts of the earth. The response that Christians should give to a soon-returning King is to carry the good news of God's forgiving love to the world.

Instead of wringing our hands over the desperate situation in our world, we ought to ring the dinner bell, inviting the human race to God's banquet of forgiveness and love. It will be too late to work for him when he returns; if we are going to win people to Christ, if we are going to lift burdens from mankind, if we are going to minister in the society where we live, let's do it now. The night is coming when no man can work. In other words, let us make hay while the Son shines.

So many of God's people are busy about peripheral matters. I hear so many church members say that they have no time to work in the church and for the coming King.

And many believers think that they cannot serve unless they engage in some colorful activity in the church, such as singing in the choir, teaching a class, or leading in the building program. But Jesus glorified the common work that Christians can contribute in our time. In Matthew 10:42, he told us that not even a cup of cold water, given in his name, would be forgotten. Jesus glorified the insignificant. The Lord did not call us to be flashy, but to be faithful. So when you serve the Lord in your small capacity, when you grapple with the babies in the nursery, when you work on the bus rounding up children who would not come otherwise, when you work in the kitchen in the church, when you keep records in a small class, when you donate your time to take care of little ones in a day school, when you contribute a few hours with a sick person or a senior citizen, all of these are noticed by him who saw a little woman toss two mites into the collection plate and reminded us that the sacrificial gift of that little woman was greater than the resounding amounts donated by the rich out of their abundance.

I hear people talk about "the good old days," and I know that there were some advantages in the past. But this is the greatest time to be alive and to be able to serve in the kingdom of God. There are more people now than ever before. In 1860, the earth's population reached a billion. Now, in the 1980s, we have four billion, and by 2000 AD, if the Lord tarries, there will be eight billion. What a challenge. The harvest is truly plenteous, but the laborers, the workers, people who are willing to sweat for Jesus, are few. There are more souls to be saved, more bodies to be fed, more hearts to be comforted, more tears to be dried, more burdens to be lifted than ever before. Christians, let's get busy. Onward, Christian soldiers! The time is short!

These days are full of opportunity, not only because of the population explosion, but because there are more instruments with which to serve. This is the day of the mass media. We have television, radio, newspapers, and books galore. This is golden opportunity for proclaiming the gospel to every creature and fulfilling the Great Commission. I am grateful for the past; I thank God for Moody and Sunday and Sam Jones and Gipsy Smith and all the great who served so nobly in years gone by. But they were limited; they couldn't travel the way we do; they couldn't communicate the way we do. Billy Graham, in one of his television presentations, talks to more people in one night than Moody spoke to in a lifetime.

The King is coming. This is no time to loaf; this is no time to lounge on the bench; this is no time to sit. But so many of God's people are playing church. We cannot win the world without work, and we cannot produce the work without people. So God needs you, and he wants to bless the world through you and me.

God's service is reasonable service. God is not asking us to do things beyond our scope or strength. Every Christian could win at least one person a year to Jesus. What would break and bankrupt other businesses would spell success for the church. If a car salesman sold only one car a year, he couldn't survive. If an insurance salesman sold one policy a year, he couldn't make it. If a real estate agent sold just one house a year, he'd go broke. And yet what would bring failure to other enterprises would be a victory for the church of God. Let's get busy.

The coming of Jesus always leads to service and character. This consoling truth that our Lord is coming soon is linked with everything good and practical in the Bible. In 1 John 3:1-3, the writer is talking about the Lord's return, and he concludes his exposition by telling us that if we entertain this hope, it should make a difference in our lives because we would purify ourselves, even as God is pure. Second Peter 3:11, after the apostle has described the cataclysmic results of the Lord's return, exhorts us that in the light of this truth we should change the way we talk and the way we live.

So let's work till Jesus comes. And when we have fought our last battle, wept our last tear, preached our last sermon, prayed our last prayer, sung our last song, lifted our last burden, we can hear our returning King say, "Well done, thou good and faithful servant."

6
Something Beautiful

Brethren, my heart's desire and prayer to God for Israel is, that they might be saved. For I bear them record that they have a zeal of God, but not according to knowledge. For they being ignorant of God's righteousness, and going about to establish their own righteousness, have not submitted themselves unto the righteousness of God. For Christ is the end of the law for righteousness to every one that believeth. (Romans 10:1-4)

The most beautiful thing that can happen to a human being is to become a child of God. No other experience in human existence can compare to that. If you become successful in business and amass a fortune, it will not be comparable to the moment that you were saved. If your name becomes a household word, and you are recognized everywhere, it will not approximate the miracle that happens when you receive Jesus. If you excel intellectually and harvest a crop of prestigious degrees from the best universities in the world, it will not be in the class of linking your freedom to the grace of God.

It is beautiful because it fills the life of the believer with love, joy, and peace. Drugs and pleasures, money and fame cannot do that for a person. We should not have to beg people to accept a Christ who fills the life with forgiving love and then become one's partner from salvation to physical death, and then into eternity. And this friend does not run for cover when the going gets difficult. He is a "friend that sticketh closer than a brother," and he promised that he would never leave us or forsake us. Life is not worthwhile without a sense of meaning; that is why so many in our culture are looking for it, and they cannot find it.

This reminds me of the well-known story of the little boy who got a nice guitar for Christmas. He put his hands on the fret and held it in a fixed position while he strummed on the instrument by the hour. His father became vexed with him and said, "Son, you are supposed to move your left hand up and down the fret and produce new sounds. Chet Atkins and Les Paul, the great guitarists, do that." The little boy replied, "Well, Dad, they run their left hand up and down because they are looking for it—I found it." And when you come to Jesus and accept the gift of eternal life, you have found it.

The beautiful part about this wonderful experience is that it is a gift of God to undeserving sinners. Everything good in life costs something, often very much. If you want a good education, you have to invest hours of laborious effort to achieve your goal. If you want to become a good athlete, you have to pay the price of practice and even suffering. If you want to excel in the field of business, you must discipline yourself and spend a lot of time to fulfil your dreams. But the grace of God is a gift from God. It cost us forty billion dollars to put a man on the moon; it is going to cost us one hundred billion dollars to put a man on Mars (if we ever do), but we can put a man in heaven for nothing.

Some years ago a young couple called me excitedly to tell me that they were going to Hawaii. The husband was a salesman, and he had won a free trip for two because of his expertise in selling. I congratulated them and rejoiced with them. But when I hung up the phone, I thought to myself, "Why should they be so excited?" That was wonderful, but I pass out free trips to Heaven every time I get up to preach. Why don't people get excited about that? A trip to Hawaii is temporary, but when God gives us a free trip to heaven, it is forever.

And this beautiful package of salvation is an absolute. Everyone gets the same blessing of eternal life. There are no VIPs in salvation. A little boy coming down the aisle this week to be saved is just as saved as Billy Graham. The dying thief on the cross who accepted Christ is just as saved as Mary, the virgin mother of our

Savior. And because of its absolute nature, there is no way you diminish salvation or increase it.

In our text, Paul is talking about this beautiful miracle. No one had a better insight into the grace of God than the apostle. Most men have to be saved from their badness—Paul had to be saved from his goodness. In Philippians 3:6, he tells us that concerning the law, he was blameless. He was zealous for Judaism, he was a Pharisee, he was a moral man of high standing, and yet on the road to Damascus, something beautiful happened to him. And he began to share it everywhere. He said in Romans 9:3 that he was willing to go to hell in order that his brethren in the flesh, the Jews, might be saved. There is no greater compassion than that. And this passage defines this "something" that can happen to you in this service if you are willing to furnish the sinner and let God furnish the Savior.

In the verses of our text, Paul talks about this beautiful salvation. He gives us a definition, and he approaches the task by exploding three popular misconceptions that were prevalent in his day. In Paul's time, as in ours, many had false notions as to what constituted salvation. So in verses 1-3, Paul tells us what salvation is not, and then in verse four he spells out the true meaning of God's amazing grace.

We Are Not Saved by Race (verse 1)

Paul begins by telling us that we are not saved by *race*. He is talking to his "brethren," and he tells them that the deep desire in his heart and the principal burden of his prayers is that Israel might be saved. I am sure that when Paul said this everyone in the audience gasped. You see, it was a popular misconception that Jews were automatically saved. They were children of Abraham, they were the possessors of the Law, they were the object of the covenants, they had produced the great prophets in the past; salvation was not for them. Salvation was all right for the pagan, for the Gentile, for the outsider, but the Jews were exempt, or so they thought. But Paul affirms that they need to be saved, and that their national heritage does not automatically make them sons of God.

Paul was teaching that we are not saved by race—we are saved by grace. Paul was saying that we are not saved by generation, but regeneration. We are not saved by chromosomes; we are saved by Calvary. We are not saved by genes; we are saved by Golgotha. Redemption cannot be passed down from one generation to the next. One can leave money to the next generation; one can leave a family business or a family name to others, but the grace of God cannot be conveyed in this way.

Did you ever stop to realize that God has no grandchildren? Some of you grandparents may feel sorry for God about this. People with grandchildren love to talk about these precious miracles. A man walked up to one of his friends and said, "Have I told you about my grandchildren?" The friend replied, "No, and I sure do appreciate it." But in God's family everyone has to be born again.

I have two sons, but the fact that they were born into a preacher's home does not automatically make them sons of God. At the age of seven, both of them accepted Christ. And now, though I am their physical father, they are my spiritual brothers. My own sons are my brothers! Everyone has to be born again. Salvation is not optional. It's a divine imperative. God commands all men everywhere to repent. The entire human race needs to be saved by grace. And these Jews had to realize that being born into a chosen race did not save them automatically. In fact, John the Baptist became so irate at that popular misconception that he pointed to a bunch of rocks and said, "God can take these stones and raise up children unto Abraham" (Matthew 3:9). The Jews had been bragging about not needing repentance because they were the sons of Abraham.

Some years ago I was in an airport between planes, and I fell into a chance conversation with a businessman. I asked him, "Are you a Christian?" He looked at me real funny and replied, "Of course, I am a Christian; what do you think I am, a heathen? I was born in America, and America is a Christian country—therefore I am a Christian." I had to say to this man, "Friend, being born in a Christian country does not make you a Christian any more than being born in a garage would make you an automobile." External advantages do not produce internal spirituality. But so many people have the idea that familial advantages make them exempt from the salvation that is needed by everyone. This concept is still current in our day. But it has no value in the sight of God. If men could be saved this way, Jesus would not have died on the cross, but he assures us that he is the only true way, and that no man can come to the Father but by him (John 14:6).

I heard a black preacher say that because a mother cat had kittens in the oven, that did not make them biscuits! That is a graphic way of saying that location and environmental advantages do not change the inner man in the sight of God. Let us not forget that the Infinite is perfect and he requires perfection, and we do not have that perfection, and it can be furnished to us as a gift through the grace of God. That is why everyone, rich or poor, educated or illiterate, cultured or uncultured must receive the gift of divine forgiveness.

The Apostle Paul, who is speaking here, had racial advantages that were superb. In Philippians 3:5 he talks about this genetic legacy that he inherited. He was a Hebrew of the Hebrews, he was of the tribe of Benjamin, one of the greatest tribes among the Jews, he was circumcised on the eighth day, he was of the stock of Israel, and yet in 1 Corinthians 15:10 he could say that the only thing which made his life important was the grace of God. He did not glory in his background, education, or devotion to the Jewish tradition. His sole boast was in the cross of Jesus Christ (Gal. 6:14).

We Are Not Saved by Religion (verse 2)

Not only are we not saved by race, we are not saved by religion. In verse 2, Paul states that the Jew has a zeal of God, but not according to knowledge. The Hebrew was very religious. He was not an atheist, and not only did he believe in God, but he was zealous in his faith. But religion does not save. Religion is what we do for God; Christianity is what God, in Christ, has done for us. Religion is man looking for God. Christianity is God looking for man. The world of our day trusts in religion. Many belong to some church or subscribe to some creed. And modern man thinks that he is acceptable in the sight of God because he has "faith" of some sort. But it is possible to come to God the wrong way. Paul called it "not according to knowledge." It is not enough to come to God—we must come the right way. Cain came to the Lord, and he did not deny His existence or question his need of a higher power, but he approached God incorrectly, and so many are doing this in our day.

I'm amazed when I encounter many who think that because they believe in a supreme being they have nothing to worry about. James 2:19 states that the devils believe in God and tremble. There is no atheism among demons. Some of the greatest statements in the Scripture concerning the power of God and the person of Christ come from devils and demons. Only man is foolish enough to be an atheist. "The fool hath said in his heart there is no God" (Ps. 14:1). But members of the unseen world have seen the divine power in operation. They have seen the footprints of God in creation and in the transformation of human personality. They surveyed the power of Christ in his earthly ministry and perceived his deity in healing the sick and mending broken hearts and raising the dead, and they have deduced from these events the reality of a supreme deity.

Did you ever stop to realize that you can reject Christ by joining a church? Many in our day, instead of repenting of their sinful and broken nature and admitting that they cannot save themselves, try to resolve the problem by affiliating with a church. And do not misunderstand me, every believer should be a member of a church and be involved, not merely on the roll. But the Word of God does not teach salvation by church membership. The fact that you are a Baptist or a Methodist or a Catholic does not mean that you are a member of the family of God. Church membership is essential after you are saved; it is not a condition for salvation.

I have a minister friend who one day was standing in a hotel lobby. A man approached him and said, "Are you a minister?" My friend replied in the affirmative. The stranger inquired further, "What church?" My friend answered, "I'm a Baptist." The man said, "Oh, you are a Baptist; you are a member of that narrow, narrow church that believes only your gang is going to heaven." The preacher replied, "You are mistaken. I am more narrow than that. I don't believe that some of my gang are going to make it." So you are not saved because you belong to a church or submit to some creed, no matter how orthodox. The issue is a person, the Lord Jesus Christ, who alone can do for you what you cannot do for yourself.

The false foundation that religious pretensions often provoke are responsible for a person's unwillingness to face himself and admit that he needs to become a new creature in Christ. The Pharisees were guilty of this, and Christ warned them of this danger. In Matthew 21:31, Jesus told these good moral and religious men that the publicans and the harlots would go to heaven ahead of them. Jesus was not glorifying immorality or moral looseness; he was simply implying that those moral derelicts were aware of their condition, but the stubborn Pharisees were employing substitutes for salvation and were unwilling to admit their need.

The little boy was playing alone; he had his ball and bat and was throwing the ball into the air and trying to hit it. He must have thrown the ball and missed at least ten times. An old man, standing and watching, was amused at the boy's antics. Finally, he said to him, "Son, you are not a very good hitter, are you?" The boy replied, "No, but I'm a doggone good pitcher." That same attitude is prevalent in our day among so many. We are not willing to admit our failure and find the answer in the grace of God.

Religion is dangerous, not only in deceiving us concerning eternity, but in not providing solutions for the problems and heartaches that we confront in this life. We live in a hurting world, and the aspirin of religion cannot do what the surgery of salvation and true faith can accomplish. Walter Winchell said that for every light that shines on Broadway, there is a broken heart to match it. We live in a world of broken hearts, and only the solution that genuine faith in Christ can bring is the only way that life can be meaningful and worthwhile. Dear friend, don't bank on substitutes. There is a balm in Gilead. "The Great Physician now is near, the sympathizing Jesus." He who made the universe, and lit the sun, and gave the stars their celestial push, and placed them in their orbit can stoop into your broken life and fill it with peace, joy, and love.

We Are Not Saved by Right Living (verse 3)

Many in our day are facing the same situation. They think that God is an accountant, and every time they do something good they think God puts it down on the right-hand side of the ledger, and every time that they do something bad he puts it down on the left-hand side. And then he adds them up when they die. If the good deeds exceed the bad ones, you go to heaven, and if the bad deeds exceed the good ones, you go to hell. Nothing is farther from the truth than that. Man is not saved by human effort, and God is not an accountant.

Please understand me. Loving your neighbor and doing good to others is commendable, but no one is saved like that. Mothers, do not say to your children that if they are good, they go to heaven, and if they are bad, they go to hell. That is wrong theology. No one is going to heaven for being good; no one is going to hell for being bad. People are going to heaven because they accept Christ as Savior; they are going to hell because they reject Christ as Savior. Salvation is an act of the will, not a mode of behavior. Paul reminds us that we are saved by the goodness of God, not by human goodness, and it is not based on works; it is a gift, and all you can do with a gift is to extend empty hands and receive it (Eph. 2:8-9).

The best person in the world still has to kneel at the foot of the cross and say, "God, be merciful to me a sinner." Call the roll: resurrect Mary, the virgin mother of our Savior, Paul, Simon Peter, Francis of Assisi; Dwight L. Moody, and compound their goodness into one person. That individual would not be acceptable in the sight of a perfect God. God cannot accept human goodness; it is not enough. That is why Paul could say in Titus 3:5 that our works of righteousness cannot regenerate us.

I am not disparaging humane behavior. Doing good works and helping our fellowman should be the order of the day for everyone. But, you know, a good thing can became horrible by not using it correctly. Take, for example, hair combing. If I were to say, "I am tired of breathing; I have been breathing for fifty-eight years, day in day out, and I am tired of breathing. From now on, instead of breathing, I am going to comb hair." Now what is wrong with hair combing? Not a thing. Everyone should comb his hair, if he has some. With some men the hair turns white—with others it turns loose. But if you have hair you ought to comb it. But hair combing is no substitute for breathing. If you stop breathing and comb hair instead, you have made hair combing murder, self murder. And a good thing, hair combing, has become horrible and sinful because you have tried to make it do what it was never meant to do, replace breathing.

So, being good is wonderful and doing kind deeds is commendable, but they are no substitute for what Christ did for the human race on the rugged cross. If you try to substitute good works for divine salvation, you are making good works the worst form of bad works. You are making goodness into soul murder, and a good thing has become horrible because human goodness, wonderful in the horizontal direction, toward our fellowman, was never meant to take the place of the love that wrought salvation's plan and the cross that brought it down to man.

That is what Paul meant in Galatians 2:22 when he said that he did not frustrate the grace of God, but if salvation comes by human effort, by the Law, then Christ died unnecessarily. The death of Jesus is a mere appendage if man can be saved by the works of the Law. Even in the Garden of Gethsemane, Jesus asked his Heavenly Father that if salvation could be accomplished some other way, to let the cup of the crucifixion pass from him. But Jesus went to the cross to remind us that there is no other way. The cross remains a mute testimony throughout the ages that salvation by human effort is void. You cannot be saved that way; you must come by the way of the cross; there is no other way under heaven or among men whereby we must be saved (Acts 4:12).

So, dear friend, why don't you admit that a divine intervention is the only solution to your situation. Why languish in the throes of uncertainty when the Blessed Savior has gone to the tree for you and for me. Your good works will be meaningful only as you use them as the proof of salvation and an expression of gratitude for what Christ has done for you.

We Are Saved by a Redeemer (verse 4)

We are not saved by race or by religion or by right living. Now Paul comes to the positive affirmation—we are saved by a Redeemer. Salvation is not a plan—it is a person. Our redemption is rooted in the love of a Savior. Christ is the end of the Law, for salvation, or righteousness to every one that believeth. He who created the universe, he who was born in a manger, he who went to a cross and paid for our sins, he who ascended into heaven forty days after his resurrection, he who sits at the right hand of God the Father and has been doing this for 2,000 years, he who will come again without sin unto salvation is the One who saves us sinful human beings.

You remember that heaven named Jesus before he was born. In Matthew 1:21 the angel told Mary to call his name Jesus because he would save his people from their sins. He did not say that he would save them from poverty, as wonderful as that would have been. He did not say that he would save his people from ignorance, as wonderful as education is. The root problem of the human race is sin, and that is what Jesus came to solve. Man cannot handle his sins. He might do a little about his ignorance or about his financial position or about his environmental setting, but he can do nothing about his sins. It takes a miracle to grapple with human iniquity. And in the mystery of the cross, on that Friday afternoon, Jesus paid for the sins of the human race (John 1:29).

Let us not forget that people were saved in the Old Testament like we are saved now, through Christ. They were saved by looking forward to his coming; we are saved by looking backward on his advent. Their faith was prophetic; ours is historical. They looked to the future, and we look to the past. There are not two plans of salvation, one for the folks before Christ and one for those after Christ. Salvation, BC and AD, is the same. Jesus is "the author and the finisher of our faith." "In him we live and move and have our being."

You recall Paul's exhortation to Timothy in 2 Timothy 3:15 where the apostle reminded his young friend how he was saved. He told him that as a child he had been taught the Holy Scriptures, or the Old Testament, where he discovered that salvation came by faith in Christ. And, mind you, he learned about Jesus from the Old Testament; for when Paul was writing 2 Timothy, the New Testament had not yet been written. So he was referring to the Old Testament as the source of his information about salvation, and it centered in Christ.

There is an interesting insight in Hebrews 11:23-26. Paul was talking about Moses, the great prophet and patriarch of the Old Testament. And he affirmed that Moses did business with Jesus when he decided to turn his back on the riches of Egypt and the comforts of being a member of royalty. And he chose to suffer afflictions with the people of God, rather than to enjoy the pleasures of sin for a season. He considered the reproach of Christ (and this was hundreds of years before Jesus was born) greater riches than the wealth of Egypt. In other words, Moses looked at the treasures of Egypt and the riches of being in Christ, and he said, "I'd rather have Jesus." So Moses, in the Old Testament, dealt with Jesus in his decision to do the will of God.

In Galatians 3:22 there is another intriguing statement about salvation in the Old Testament. It states that the Scripture (the Old Testament) describes the entire human race "under sin"; we are all guilty of transgressions. What is the purpose of this condemnation? The next line tells us "that the promise by faith of Jesus Christ might be given to them that believe." So there is the universal condemnation of all men, and the subsequent miracle that can happen through Jesus to every one that believeth. That is the plan of salvation, pure and simple, and it comes from the Old Testament.

When Jesus died on the cross, he concluded his passion by saying, "It is finished" (John 19:30). Three words in English; in Spanish, in my own native tongue, it is two words, *consumado es;* in Greek, it is one, *tetelesthai.* A great Greek scholar of England contends that this is a commerical word, that Jesus lifted that word from the field of business to describe the transaction that he enacted on the cross. It is said that this word was used to cancel a bill that had been paid. If you had lived two thousand years ago, and you entered a business establishment where you owed some money, and after your creditor consulted the ledger and told you how much you owed him, and you would pay it completely, he would write across the face of your bill the same Greek word that Christ uttered on the cross, *tetelesthai*. The Greek scholar contends that a better translation, instead of "it is finished," would be "paid in full."

This is what Jesus did for every person. He took the sin bill of the human race and marked across the face of it, "paid in full," and now there is nothing against us. All we can do is to accept the finished work of Christ. Salvation comes through a redeemer who "paid it all."

7
All in the Family

There was a certain rich man, which was clothed in purple and fine linen, and fared sumptuously every day: And there was a certain beggar named Lazarus, which was laid at his gate, full of sores, And desiring to be fed with the crumbs which fell from the rich man's table: moreover the dogs came and licked his sores. And it came to pass, that the beggar died, and was carried by the angels into Abraham's bosom: the rich man also died, and was buried: And in hell he lifted up his eyes, being in torments, and seeth Abraham afar off, and Lazarus in his bosom. And he cried and said, Father Abraham, have mercy on me, and send Lazarus, that he may dip the tip of his finger in water, and cool my tongue; for I am tormented in this flame. But Abraham said, Son, remember that thou in thy lifetime receivedst thy good things, and likewise Lazarus evil things: but now he is comforted, and thou art tormented. And beside all this, between us and you there is a great gulf fixed: so that they which would pass from hence to you cannot; neither can they pass to us, that would come from thence. Then he said, I pray thee therefore, father, that thou wouldest send him to my father's house: For I have five brethren; that he may testify unto them, lest they also come into this place of torment. Abraham saith unto him, They have Moses and the prophets; let them hear them. And he said, Nay, father Abraham: but if one went unto them from the dead, they will repent. And he said unto him, If they hear not Moses and the prophets, neither will they be persuaded, though one rose from the dead.
(Luke 16:19-31)

We have before us a true story. This is not a parable. To begin with it is not introduced as a parable, and then again, names are mentioned. In parables, names are never mentioned. We have three names recorded in this narrative: Abraham, Moses, and Lazarus.

Jesus tore a page from the book of eternity and is saying to us, "This is the way it looks on the other side of the grave." The name of the rich man is not mentioned. Perhaps he had kinfolks in the audience, and Jesus did not want to hurt or embarrass them. Two men die and go in different directions and to different destinies. The wealthy man was unsaved. He was not unsaved because he was rich. Wealth does not determine our spiritual status. Many rich people are humble followers of Christ, and many poor people refuse to be saved.

The doctrine of hell is not very popular in our day. Most preachers do not deny its existence, but they just ignore it. Modern congregations rarely hear a sermon on this subject. But Jesus mentioned it frequently. In fact, he says more about hell than anyone else in the Bible. Peter, James, and John do not talk about hell with the frequency that Jesus does. If anyone knew about that dreadful place, it was the blessed Son of God. He who came to bear our sins and knew the price that he had to pay to expiate our transgressions is eligible to talk about it. If there were no hell, I believe he would have told us. But he warns us repeatedly that such a place exists, but that men and women do not have to go there, for God wills that none should perish but that all should come to repentance.

Some try to eliminate hell by saying that everybody will go to heaven, but the Bible does not teach universalism, that all people will be saved. Others tell us that there is a hell, but only the devil and his angels will be there. Others say that there is a hell and that men are going there, but they won't stay in there forever. They contend that eventually they will be released, that it is inconceivable that hell should exist forever.

Origen, the famous church father, believed that eventually even the devil and his angels would be released—he could not conceive of a dualism in eternity. He believed that God would not allow a place like hell to go on forever, contradicting the beautiful existence that shall prevail in heaven forever. All the above unbiblical opinions are based on the reason of man. The truth of the Word of God, however, rests on what God has said, not on what man senses.

The Word of God has many descriptions for hell. Here it is called a place of torment. In another place it is called a place of great anxiety, where there is "weeping and wailing and gnashing of teeth." Can you imagine being in a state of having anxiety forever with no relief? In another place hell is described as a bottomless pit. The sensation of falling forever is indescribable. Still another picture of hell is outer darkness, the soul of the sinner living in perennial darkness and in lonely isolation. Mark Twain said that he chose heaven for climate and hell for company, but there will be no fraternizing in hell. Everyone will be an island, desolate and alone. Another description of hell is a garbage dump, or "Gehenna." And that is what hell is, a place where wasted lives will reside forever. A man without Christ has wasted his life. The fact that he is rich or famous does not give him the status of being a true human being.

But I am not going to talk about hell in this sermon; I am concerned about this family. This rich man had at least five brothers, maybe some sisters, and a father and mother. Here was a prominent family with a member in hell. Their success in time did not promote their success in eternity. It is better to fail in time and succeed in eternity than to succeed in time and fail in eternity. Of course, it is better to succeed in both. Let us note some salient features about this prominent family.

I. A Wealthy Family

The story describes this family as a wealthy family. They had scored in the field of commerce, and doubtlessly this brought them many of the comforts and notoriety that money affords. And there is nothing wrong with this. Being successful in the financial field is certainly not a curse. God does not condemn success or elevate poverty to a virtue. Some of the greatest men in the Bible were very successful. David, the man after God's own heart, was a rich man. Abraham, who was described as the friend of God, was a wealthy man. Job, before his calamities struck, was one of the richest men of that area. Solomon, the colorful king of Israel, was a man of tremendous opulence. Joseph of Arimathaea, who supervised the burial of our Lord, was considered a man of means. When money has been earned in a legitimate way, and the wealthy person uses it to help others, money can be a blessing.

Jesus never condemned wealth or material things per se. He deplored the fact that often men would allow secondary things to take the place of the more important aspects of life. This is always a sin, and this is what the devil tries to do to people who are successful, to major on minors and to put second things first. In Matthew 6:19 Jesus talked about laying up treasures in heaven. He instructed men not to lay up things upon the earth where they are temporary, where moth and rust corrupt and thieves break through and steal. Notice that Jesus did not destroy the passion for possession, but he said that we should be careful where we put our wealth. He did not say that we shouldn't lay up any treasures at all, but he was concerned that we store them in heaven, or give them a spiritual repository.

We are instructed in 2 Timothy 2:9 that "the love of money is the root of all evil." But notice that Paul did not say that money was the root of all evil, but rather the love of money or the worship of money was the root of all evil. In passing, I think it appropriate to note that the word for "love" in this verse is the word *agape*. This is the love that you show toward God and vice versa. So the apostle was telling us not to love money the way we love God, or not to make a god out of material things. I meet so many businessmen who are doing just this, and woe and misery will be the ultimate result of that practice. God never intended that we worship the dollar and devote our major energies to it. This can be a curse to our health and to our family and to our nation.

So we should not deny the benefits of money and the blessings that it can confer when properly used. Nor should we deify money and put it in a place where it does not belong, but we ought to dedicate money to serve others and to bring honor and glory to the name of the Lord.

Despite the fact that material things can render a great service, they cannot satisfy the deeper needs of the human heart. Money may buy an education, but it will not buy wisdom. Money may buy a house, but it won't buy a home. Money may buy acquaintances, but it won't buy friendship. Money may buy marriage, but it won't buy love. Money may buy medical attention, but it won't buy health. Money may buy thrills, but it won't buy happiness. That is why men should realize the limitations of the material, and not put it in first place. It is sinful to assign money a position that it does not merit. We all know that it is temporary. When sickness comes, money does not count for much. We often say about money that we cannot take it with us. Groucho Marx said that you cannot take it with you; it goes before you do. Inflation, depression, tragedy, business catastrophes can make money ineffective.

When Alexander the Great, the marvelous ruler of Greece who expired at age 33, was dying, he called his leaders together and made a request. He told them that he was going to die, and he asked his friends to bury him in a casket that had two holes, one on each side. He instructed his aids that, when they placed him in this coffin, they pull his hands through the holes. As his cortege went down the streets of Athens, he wanted his subjects to see that even though he ruled and owned the world, he was going out emptyhanded.

Money can secure many favors for us among men; it can furnish entrance into select groups of prominent people, but it will not have any bearing in eternity. George Pullman, the railroad millionaire, passed away suddenly. His funeral was very lavish. They secured the most ornate coffin that money could buy. His church service was attended by dignitaries from around the world who came to pay their last respects. The report goes that the music was stirring and unforgettable. The preacher who officiated, a great orator, composed melodic words about Pullman's life and good deeds. The long procession moved slowly to a prominent burying place. The workers had prepared his final resting place in a sea of flowers. They lowered the coffin into the grave. They covered it with flowers and filled it with cement. They placed some soil on the top, and a beautiful marble monument at the head. But when the judgment day comes, that gilded sarcophagus will burst like the shell of an egg, and George Pullman will stand before his Maker to be judged on the same basis as the porter who swept out his trains.

According to the Scriptures, this rich man had everything that money could buy in this life. And what is true about him, was no doubt true of the entire family. Maybe much of his money had come from his father, who helped him get started, and also the other members of the family. The man feasted sumptuously every day. He did not have steak just once in a while. He had it for breakfast, dinner, and supper, every day. His clothing was expensive. He wore purple and fine linen. According to biblical commentators, this was the attire used by the high priest. Only the wealthy could afford to dress like that.

II. A Weeping Family

This family was not only a wealthy family, but it was a weeping family. Their brother had died. We do not know if it was a sudden death, like a stroke or a heart attack, or whether he lingered as a sick man for many months and suffered before he died. The death could have been accidental and therefore sudden; the record does not describe this aspect. But deaths in the family are always heart-rending. This brother could have been deeply loved by the family. From the narrative it seems that he was a winsome human being, as we shall see later. But he was dead. And one can hear the sound of weeping and the muffled sobs among those wealthy brothers and their mother and father. Let us not forget that the rich can cry. Sorrow is no respecter of persons. The rich and the poor, the good and the bad, the educated and the illiterate, the high and the low all have tear ducts that release their liquid contents when a loved one passes on.

God never promised to release any one of us from the experience of sorrow and despair. The highway of life is littered with disaster from the cradle to the grave. Daniel suffered, David suffered, Jeremiah suffered, the father of the Prodigal Son suffered, and even the Son of God looked up from the old rugged cross and asked, "My God, my God, why?" So the presence of sorrow is to be found everywhere. If it isn't one thing, it will be another. Some will have trouble with money—they cannot make ends meet. Others will have physical problems and will suffer with sickness and chronic ailments. Others will have trouble in the home. A mother and father cannot get along, and they rupture their relationship and impose indescribable suffering upon their children. Others have trouble with wayward sons and daughters; they spend their days and nights in anguish because of the prodigal ways of young people whom they love dearly. So brace yourself. The dark hour is going to come.

And sometimes the difficult hour will wait until the last of life. I have a friend who seemed to have an ideal situation in every way. He grew up in a lovely home and married a beautiful girl with money, charm, and a delightful family. In business everything he touched turned to gold. Beautiful children began to come into his home. They were well, healthy, and brilliant in school. They received the best education that money could buy; they lived lives that brought joy and happiness to the parents. In the early years of his life, this friend had no problems—no surgery, no sickness. He was a picture of health. Then one day, in his senior years, he detected a pain in the abdomen. For the first time he went to a hospital for extensive tests. It was cancer. He languished for many months in pain, and death finally came and released him from his misery. But it was late in life that he confronted his dark hour, and to each one of us the shadow and the tears are going to come in some form, sooner or later.

No one is special in the game of life. Money, education, fame, and fortune are not deterrents to suffering and heartache. That is why you need God. The circumstances are bigger than you are. You are no match for the status quo. We all need strength from above. We need someone to walk with us when we stare death in the face. We need someone who stands with us. We need someone who will never leave us or forsake us. And Jesus is the One who can stand by our side and say, "Let not your heart be troubled." I like the line in Isaiah that says about our Lord that he was "a man of sorrows and acquainted with grief." And because he has walked with sorrow and is conversant with the content of the dark hour, he can be a high priest who can be touched with the feeling of our infirmities.

III. A Wicked Family

Not only was this a wealthy family and a weeping family, but it was a wicked family. They left God out of their lives. They had no sky in their world; they lived for the present and the material. They had time for money and time for pleasure and time for the secular, but they had no time for God. So many are living like that in our day. In our beloved country you will find people who are wrapped up in this present world. They have never realized that life is more than material things, and that "man shall not live by bread alone, but by every word that proceedeth out of the mouth of God." This insensitive spirit has laid the foundation for all of the misery that afflicts our generation. The wars and the broken homes and the torn hearts find their origin in this attitude. God made us for more than this, and we cheat ourselves when we concern ourselves with the evanescent, when we sacrifice the eternal upon the altar of the temporal.

You recall that Christ characterized the last days in this manner. He said that in the last days it would be like it was in the days of Noah, and Sodom and Gomorrha. They were eating and drinking in the days of Noah, and they were marrying and giving in marriage until the flood came and destroyed them all. And in the days of Sodom, they were buying and selling and building until the fire fell from heaven and consumed them (Luke 17:26-28). You will notice that these activities are not basically sinful; they are commendable and necessary. The wickedness of these people was based upon the fact that this was all that they were doing. They had no concern for the spiritual. They were involved in mundane activities; they were consumed with secular pursuits. Their time and talent was invested only in the passing and temporary phases of life. This is wickedness of the worst sort.

So this family was wicked in this sense. The rich man told Abraham that he had five brothers, and he told the patriarch that they were all afflicted with the same life-style. They were concerned only in making money and living for this present world

(Luke 16:27-28). What a tragedy, and yet this describes so many in our day "whose God is their belly," as Paul said of the Cretans, and who lie in the lap of the devil. Is this your problem, my friend? And is it possible you think that because you are not involved in something extremely wicked that you are in good shape? It may be that you use some of your money to do good for others, and you think that because you balance your spiritual negligence with token service to your fellowman that God will accept it as a substitute for your spiritual responsibility.

If you will notice in our story, this man and his family are not accused of being flagrant in their conduct. It does not say, as it does of the Prodigal Son, that this man wasted his substance in riotous living. His wickedness did not consist of immoral aberrations, but there are many kinds of wickedness, and the fleshly kind which we call sinful may be the least reprehensible to God. Jesus told the moral Pharisees "that the drunkards and the harlots would go to heaven ahead of them" (Matthew 21:31). Our Savior was not putting a premium on sinful conduct, but he was simply teaching that there are varieties of wickedness, and the Pharisees, who were substituting human goodness for divine righteousness, were all the guiltier.

In fact, it is possible that this man and his family were basically humane and good in their treatment of others. This rich man allowed the poor man to beg at his gate. He did not have to do that; Lazarus, covered with sores, did not make a pretty picture, and the wealthy man could have insisted that he, with his ugly appearance, not litter his front gate where all of his prominent visitors entered. But he permitted the beggar to sit there. More than that, he gave permission for Lazarus to eat the crumbs that fell from his table. Some Bible students contend that these crumbs were napkins, that the Greek word means that. Let us not forget that in the world of two thousand years ago, there were no knives and forks. People ate with their hands. After a few bites, the hands would become soiled, and the rich would use pieces of bread to wipe their hands and then throw them on the floor. This is probably what Lazarus ate.

The phrase, "moreover the dogs licked his sores," can also

mean that the rich man was providing medical help for Lazarus. Those dogs were not stray dogs. If you please, they were medical dogs. In that ancient day, physicians noticed that when dogs got into a fight and broke their skin, they would lick it, and healing would ensue rapidly. They deduced that there must be an antiseptic agent in the saliva of the dog and they were correct. So doctors would encourage wealthy people to keep dogs around to lick sores and wounds, and these were the dogs that worked on the sick man. So the rich man provided medical attention. He was a good man, but goodness is not enough. His wickedness consisted of leaving God out, and the worst form of evil is human goodness that poses as a substitute for divine righteousness.

IV. A Warned Family

Not only was it a wealthy family and a weeping family and a wicked family, but it was a warned family. When the rich man implored that Lazarus be allowed to go witness and testify to his brothers who were headed in the same direction, Abraham informed him that they had Moses and the prophets, so let them hear them. God does not leave himself without a witness. God is faithful in warning men about the danger of sin and the peril of rejecting divine love. The fairness of God is evident in every page of Holy Writ. The Bible is replete with warnings. God does not surprise men with judgment. He not only advises us of the dangers and dreadful results of sin and disobedience, he has made a way for our escape and has provided a salvation simple and effective within the reach of every one of us.

This rich man who went to hell is a case in point. Has it ever occurred to you that he knew the plan of salvation? He begged Abraham to tell Lazarus to urge his five brothers to "repent." He knew the way. Someone had told him. It is possible that Lazarus witnessed to him. Among his friends, there might have been those who reminded him of his spiritual responsibility. Surely, the goodness of God should have led him to repentance. He was the object of many blessings, and he had money, friends, family, and health. Surely, at some point he would be reminded that these came from God, who is "the giver of every good and perfect gift, and who is the father of lights in whom there is no variableness and shadow of turning."

So it is with many of you who are reading now. God has been good to you. These blessings ought to be a warning and an encouragement to move in the direction of accepting Christ as your Savior. You have basked in the sunshine of God's love. He has surrounded you with benefits of every kind. The oxygen and the nitrogen and the water and the sunshine are all blessings that make life possible and good. The only way to say "Thank You" is to kneel at the foot of the cross and accept his forgiveness and the gift of eternal life. This should not be difficult for you. You accept all the other gifts mentioned. Why not accept his salvation? God would rather that you reject his oxygen and his nitrogen and his water and his sunshine than to reject his Son.

And God is willing to give you what you need and cannot obtain on your own merits. Warnings galore have been introduced into your life. You need sight, not more light. A blind man needs sight, and all the light in the world cannot cause him to see. And so with you—you need sight and only Jesus can give you that. Every fragrant flower points you to the Lily of the Valley; every stone along the road points to the Rock of Ages. Every astral body in the heavens declares that the Bright and Morning Star will be your guide, if only you are willing. Every tolling of the hour, every tick of the clock is telling you to accept Christ now. There is no excuse. The warnings are profuse. God has called you again and again all of your life. His warnings are true. He does not use them to scare you; he uses them to arouse a needed action in your life. Prepare to meet thy God. It is appointed unto man once to die; the judgment is coming; now is the accepted time. All of these warnings are based on love because you can never know the peace of God until you heed the admonitions of the Word of God.

Oh, but so few are willing to heed the warning. In Noah's day only eight people obeyed and entered the ark. In the day of Sodom and Gomorrah, only a few people escaped the judgment on that city. In Luke 18:8 Jesus wondered, when he returned, if he would find faith on the earth. Oh, don't be in hell when the saints go marching in. Heed the warning. Don't be like the man in our text who wouldn't listen, and then in hell he wished that he had, and wished that his brothers would accept the warning. There is time left for you. You have the present moment in which to act. Now!

8
Guess Who's Coming to Dinner

Behold, I stand at the door, and knock: if any man hear my voice, and open the door, I will come in to him, and will sup with him, and he with me. (Revelation 3:20)

The Lord desires that every person should be saved. When a person dies without Christ, he is contradicting the wish of God for that individual. God is "not willing that any should perish, but that all should come to repentance." Jesus went to a cross to make it possible for everyone to be saved. There is no excuse for remaining in a doomed condition. And though it cost God the crucifixion of his Son in order to redeem unworthy sinners, God was willing to pay the price. Redemption cost him more than creation. God spoke worlds into existence. By fiat he created the cosmos and put the stars in their courses and populated the earth with animals of every kind and color, but he could not speak salvation into existence. It took the blood of his only begotten Son, because we could not be redeemed by corruptible things like silver and gold—we could be saved only by the death of Jesus on the tree.

The Book of Revelation gives us a panoramic view of history from the time of Jesus until the consummation of history, and even into eternity. In chapter 1 the author describes the majestic Christ in all of his power and as Savior and coming King. In chapters 2 and 3, we have a sweep of the church age. The seven churches describe conditions upon the earth between the ascension and the rapture. In chapters 4-19 we have delineation of the events that will transpire during seven years; Bible students call this the tribulation period. It will be a time of great persecution and suffering, and paradoxically, it will be a great time of salvation, for many shall come to know Christ during this period. Then in chapter 19, Jesus comes again with his church and terminates the battle of Armageddon which has been raging and involving the leading nations of the world. In chapter 20, we have a picture of the judgment of the unsaved dead, and the concluding two chapters describe the Holy City and the eternal state.

After John depicts the condition of the Laodicean church, he has Jesus knocking on the door and asking admission. The Lord of the church is standing on the outside begging for the door to open. And what is true with reference to the church also holds true with reference to human life. He is on the outside, and he wants to enter our lives and make them meaningful and worthwhile. I want to call your attention to three interesting points; first, the Dinner; second, the Diner; third, the Door.

I. The Dinner

Salvation is represented as a festive occasion. The devil has done his utmost to give the impression that salvation is a dull affair. But the Word of God constantly links the redemptive experience to joy and peace and love. Why should we be despondent when we know that our citizenship is in heaven, and our names have been written in the Lamb's book of life? Jesus said that we would sup with him, and he would sup with us. And that is what it means to be a Christian, to have warm fellowship with Jesus.

To be sure many Christians contradict this glorious truth by living lives that are depressed and defeated. But this is not caused by salvation. Rather, it is provoked by our lack of application of the great spiritual resources that are available to every believer. Jesus has provided us with grace to meet the difficult hour; he has given us instruction about what to do with situations that are complex. We need to apply these spiritual techniques to the details of life. God does not want his servants to wear a face as long as a saxophone, as I heard one preacher say. Our faces should be like the face of a clock; not marking twenty to four, but ten till two.

You remember David, the sweet singer of Israel who was called "a man after God's own heart," had an experience which reveals the nature of salvation. The Psalmist had sinned against the Lord, but he came back in Psalm 51 and confessed his wayward activity. In this penitential psalm, he cried to be clean, he begged for a spirit that was new and different. And in the midst of his petition, he asked the Lord to restore unto him the joy of his salvation. He did not ask that his salvation be restored; he was already a saved person, but the joy and the happiness were gone because he had sinned. David missed the joy because a genuine relationship with the Lord always brings an inner joy which cannot be found in the material world.

That is why salvation is called a banquet. In our text the word used is "sup," but the Greek word is *deipnon*, literally meaning a banquet, an eight-course dinner. God is not serving us a snack when he redeems us. Often, I am invited to eat a meal in a home during the revival, and I whet my appetite for something outstanding, and then when I get there, the lady of the house is sometimes serving knick knacks, little snips of this and that, nothing filling or delectable. Not so with our Savior. He prepares the best; nothing is too good for those whom he loves. The Creator and Redeemer of the universe is not skimpy in his provision. And when you come to Jesus, remember that he is going to seat you to a repast called salvation that will be unforgettable.

Let me refer again to David. In Psalm 40 he told the story of his conversion. He told us that when he was unsaved he was in a pit, he was in jail, with no freedom, but bound by the shackles of sin. He testified that the Lord lifted him out of the horrible pit and out of the miry clay. But David did not stop there; in the following verse he wrote how the Lord put his feet on the solid rock and established his goings. But the point I want to make is that he concludes the narration of his conversion by telling us that the Lord put a song in his mouth. David said that he was in the pit, in sorrow and despair, and the Lord delivered him and put a melody in his heart. In other words, the Lord pulled him out of the mire and put him in the choir. And he will do that for you and for me.

In Luke 10 the disciples had returned from an evangelistic tour.

They were rejoicing over the results. They told how they saw the dead resurrected, the sick made well, the blind see, and deaf hear. They related in glowing terms how they even saw Satan and his cohorts defeated. They beheld devils cast out of human beings. All this was a great source of joy to the disciples. Jesus listened to them patiently, and then he told them that they might well rejoice over those many accomplishments, but he reminded them that the true basis for their joy should be in the fact that their names were written in heaven (Luke 10:20). Everything else is peripheral, inconsequential, to the titanic truth that we have become children of God, and we belong to him who loves us with an everlasting love.

Why do we have to beg people to attend this banquet? That is what has stunned me for all these many years that I have been an evangelist. I am perplexed that men have to be cajoled to sit at the Lord's table and ingest the many dishes that infinite love has prepared for sinners. I can understand man's reluctance to attend this festive occasion if the Lord were inviting us to a dull affair. But God is not inviting you to a funeral when he invites you to be saved. He is not inviting you to an execution; he is not inviting you to a jail; he is insisting that you sit at his table and have a party.

In Luke 14 Jesus related a parable about a festive supper prepared by a wealthy man. And at suppertime he sent his servants to announce to those invited, "Supper's ready." It is ready—man does not have to bring anything to it. Sometimes in churches where I minister, the ladies will have a dinner, and everyone is exhorted to bring a covered dish. Some of them will furnish salads; others, meat; others, vegetables and desserts. Not so at God's banquet; all things are ready. All we have to do is to bring our appetite. Infinite grace has made ample provision for every sinner, for "whosoever will." You recall that the people in our story began to make excuses. One blamed his business; another his vocation—he had to break some steers; still a third person— he was perhaps young—gave a domestic excuse. He had married a wife and he could not attend the banquet. People are still giving excuses, irrational and unreasonable alibis. God is inviting you to a dinner. I pray that you will respond today.

II. The Diner

In our text, Jesus is standing at the door. Here is the picture of a house, the Savior is knocking, and it is up to you to respond. The Redeemer does not send anyone else. He does not send Michael or Gabriel—he comes himself. In the Bible the Lord often delegates work to angels. When he was going to announce the birth of Jesus he sent Gabriel; when he wanted the body of Moses for the transfiguration scene, he sent Michael (Jude 19). But when he wants to save sinners, he does not send others, he comes himself. Think of it. The God who made the universe, the One who died on the cross, the One who is coming again stands at the door of your life and pleads with you to accept the gift of divine love.

This gesture of Christ's coming and not sending another indicates the importance of salvation. When dignitaries come to visit our country, the president will send the vice-president or one of the members of the cabinet to greet the arriving guest. But when a very important person comes to visit, the president himself will go out to meet the incoming guest. So we are important to God. Jesus himself comes to the door and invites us to become the recipients of eternal life. If people could only realize how important it is to become a child of God. I am afraid that so many have not comprehended the dimensions that salvation covers. No wonder that Jesus insisted that it is more important to become a Christian than to gain the whole world. If one could amass all of the real estate in the world, all of its oil wells, all of its property, all of its mineral wealth, all of its business interprises and then lose his soul, he would be making a bad bargain (Matt. 16:26).

Who stands at the door? Jesus the Creator. We must not forget that the One who died on the cross created the world. Every tree, every river, every mountain, every oil deposit, every planet, every star, every constellation, every galaxy was made by him. "All things were made by him, and without him was not anything made that was made" (John 1:3). Colossians 1:16-17 teaches us that all things were made by him and for him, and that he existed before all things, and by him all things hold together. The author of Hebrews writes that God has spoken to us by his Son, and this Son is heir of all things, and by him the worlds were created.

In this day when material things are in the saddle and riding mankind, what a wonderful thing to know that the Author of the universe is inviting us to a life of victory which teaches us how to put first things first and not to major on minors. He is knocking at our door and bidding us, not only to life, but to life in abundance. God never intended for human beings merely to exist, but he invites us to live and make every moment count. He wants to hang a rainbow of hope over the cloud of human despair. There is no answer to war or poverty or sorrow or death outside of him. That is why he comes; that is why he won't leave us alone. He does not knock once and then when we fail to respond, go away. But with a divine persistence that baffles our depraved minds, the Maker of the universe insists that we open the door and allow him to bring into our lives the blessing of forgiveness, the companionship of his love, and the guarantee that beyond the confines of this limited and finite existence, we are going to spend eternity in a perfect environment.

This omnipotent Creator who stands at the door is God incarnate. He is the Infinite who became an Infant; he is the Word made flesh who dwells among us; he is the Savior wrapped in swaddling clothes; he is Emmanuel, God with us. When he was born, wise men came to visit him from the East (Matt. 2:1); when he was going to die, wise men came to visit him from the West (John 12:20). As you recall, the shepherds, the common man, also came to the manger. The shepherds came because they knew they knew nothing; the wise men came because they knew they did not know everything. These two groups still come to Jesus—those who know they know nothing, those who know they do not know everything.

But what makes it possible for him to knock on the door is the fact that this God incarnate became our Savior. His perfect life made him eligible to be our Savior and to take our sins to a cross and cancel the debt that we could not pay. Sinners are bankrupt, and they cannot save themselves. Only Jesus can do that.

I mentioned a moment ago the wise men who came from the West to visit him before he died. They had good intentions; they told Phillip that they wanted to see Jesus and talk to him. Perhaps they heard that he would be killed, and many Bible students believe that they came to offer him a teaching position in Athens. The Greeks would not kill a man simply because he was teaching something new or radical. So perhaps they wanted to make Jesus a college professor. But the Savior told these visitors that he was going to die, and when he was lifted up from the earth (and here he was referring to the crucifixion), he would draw all men unto himself. In other words, he was saying that if he died on the cross, he would put salvation on a universal level, available to all (John 12:32).

You recall that Satan tried to dissuade Jesus from dying and becoming a Savior. In the temptation after his baptism, the devil approached him in the wilderness. When Jesus hungered the devil appealed to him to turn the stones into bread. Whereas the Greeks tried to turn Jesus into a college teacher, the devil was trying to turn him into a baker (Matt. 4:3). But Jesus defeated this temptation, and he told the devil that human personality needed more than just bread or nutrition, that man needs the Word of God. Man needs a Savior, and Jesus stands at the door of our paltry existence and wants to come in. Your responsibility and mine is to let him in.

III. The Door

We have talked about the Dinner, the doctrine of a happy salvation; the Diner, the incarnate Christ who is Creator and Redeemer; and now let me conclude by discussing the Door, or the doctrine of the freedom of the will. God has given us a free will, and with that freedom we can accept or reject the offer of salvation. Calvin believed that the sovereignty of God was so operative that God would save those whom he chose to save and condemn those whom he chose to condemn, and mankind could not resist this operation. That view has often been called the doctrine of predestination or election. Calvin's extreme position is not the teaching of the Word of God, and while God is sovereign, he has chosen, in his infinite wisdom and love, to give man the choice to receive him. I like what Dwight L. Moody said, "The elect are the whosoever wills and the non-elect are the whosoever won'ts." I heard a black preacher say that in the matter of election, everybody that runs gets elected.

On the other hand, Barth, a prominent theologian, insisted that when Christ died on the cross he paid for the sins of every person, and therefore every person is saved—and mankind is not free to reject Christ. Whether he likes it or not, he is saved. This again is not taught in the Word of God. Of course, this appeals to many because it teaches universalism. Every person is going to heaven by virtue of the fact that Christ died as the Lamb of God who takes away the sins of the world. And even though we concede that the Savior died for all, and that on the cross he paid the penalty for our sins, the Bible still teaches that man has to accept Christ. The rich young ruler rejected him, and Jesus said to his own people "ye will not come unto me that ye might have life." The Gospel of John tells us that Jesus came unto his own, the Jewish people, and his own received him not (John 1:12)—they rejected him.

In the fourth chapter of John, we have the story of the woman at the well. She came at noon to draw water, and Christ engaged her in conversation about her spiritual needs and about the water of life she could drink. In so doing she would never thirst again. The woman tried to change the conversation by bring up different subjects. She injected the sex discrimination of that day; "respectable" man did not talk to a woman in public. The Lord reminded her that salvation was for both sexes, that women needed to be saved and could be. She then introduced the race problem; she informed the Savior that Jews and Samaritans had no dealings with one another. Jesus then asked her to call her husband. She informed him that she had no husband. Christ reminded her that she had been married five times, and the man that she now lived with was not her husband. You see, the woman was trying to make *religion* a matter of discussion; Jesus was trying to show her that religion is a matter of decision. The story has a happy ending; the woman received Christ and became one the best soul-winners in the Bible, but she had to open the door. Christ could not force her to be saved.

When I began preaching at the age of thirteen, I would tell a story about a famous artist who drew a beautiful picture of Christ standing at the door and knocking. There is a weary look on the face of the Master; he has been standing there waiting for a long time. He holds a lantern in His hand, and the light is burning low to indicate the patience of the Savior; he waits patiently for a response. But somebody noticed that there was not a latch on the door. Someone asked the famous painter why the latch was missing and the picture was incomplete. The artist replied that it was intentional because the latch was on the inside. And so it is: you must open the door. Christ will knock there and he has been knocking now. Every song, every prayer, every quotation from the Word of God is a knock on the door. When your baby died Jesus was knocking; when you had that car accident which almost ended your life, he was knocking. All of the blessings that you have enjoyed in life are gentle knocks on the door. Oh, open the door to him who has opened the door of heaven for you.

I heard a black preacher relate the story about a little boy who lived in a small village. The population was small, but among the inhabitants was an old man who was wise and lovable. This old man puzzled the little boy. The old man seemed to know everything. One day the little boy thought he would get the best of the wise old man. The boy caught a small bird and covered him in his hand and thought he would approach the old man and ask him if the bird, enfolded in his hand, was dead or alive. The boy figured that if the old man said "alive," he would crush the bird and present it dead; if the old man said "dead," he would open his hand and let the bird fly. So the boy saw the old man sitting under a tree and made his approach. "Old man," he said, "you know everything. I want to ask you a question. I have a bird in my hand. Is he dead or alive?" The old man looked at him for a moment, and, with a twinkle in his eye and a faint smile on his face said, "It's up to you, my boy; it's up to you." So it is up to you whether you accept Christ or reject him.

Friend, it's up to you. You have a choice. You can say yes or no to the grace of God. Say yes now; you will never regret it. I said yes to him almost a half-century ago, and I'm glad. If I could do it for you, happily would I assume this glorious privilege. But it is your door, and a nail-pierced hand is knocking there, and you must open the door. May God help you to do it now. Jesus will enter and fellowship with you and you with him.

9
Honey in the Lion

And Samson turned aside to see the carcase of the lion: and behold, there was a swarm of bees and honey in the carcase of the lion. And he took thereof in his hands, and went on eating, and came to his father and mother, and he gave them, and they did eat: but he told not them that he had taken the honey out of the carcase of the lion. (Judges 14:8,9)

    Samson is one of the most colorful characters in the Bible. His personality, his conduct, his words, and his escapades make for interesting reading. The Bible instructs us that all of these events recorded in the Old Testament have a relevant message for believers of all time. We need instruction and inspiration as we journey between the cradle and the grave. The earthly path before us is unknown, and the lives of others touch us on every side. We can learn from their mistakes and from their successes. We can apply these lessons to our own lives and benefit thereby. Everybody can teach us something, and woe unto the person who shuts his eyes to the lessons which can be learned from the experience of others. In this way they can be our benefactors, and we can compliment their lives by garnering instruction that will save us from some of the hardships through which they traversed.
    Samson was headed toward a pleasant experience. He was going to visit a girl friend. Musing along the way and looking forward to the delightful event that lay before him, suddenly the climate changed. A young lion stepped into the picture! He emerged

from the thicket into the narrow path going in the opposite direction. Samson was stunned, but he recaptured his composure, and he said, "Kitty, get out of my way, I am going to visit my girl." The lion replied, "I have a girlfriend, also, and I am on my way to see her." Neither of the antagonists would yield the road, so they got into a fight. No one knows how long the encounter lasted, but finally Samson ran his hand into the lion's mouth, then into his stomach, and grabbed his tail and turned him inside out. Having conquered his opponent (I have read between the lines a little), he disposed of him by discarding the dead carcase (carcass today) on the side of the road. Later, he passed by the same place on his trip home, and the vultures had decimated the remains of the young lion and left the skeletal part intact. Samson noticed that the bees had built a hive and were producing honey in the carcass of the lion. He took some of the honey and ate it. Then he remembered his mother and father at home and thought, "This is delicious; I think I will take some of it to my folks."

From this remarkable episode, I want to draw several lessons I trust will benefit and edify our Christian experience. First, the Conflicts of the Christian life. Second, the Confections of the Christian life. Third, the Commission of the Christian life.

I. The Conflicts of the Christian Life

Samson was on a pleasant mission; he was going to visit a female friend. Then the young lion stepped into the picture and changed everything. The Christian life is not devoid of difficult situations. The young lions are going to appear during the course of our Christian journey. God did not promise to save us from trouble when he saved us from sin. He did not promise that rainbows and sunshine and green pastures and still waters would surround our lives simply because we have received him as Savior. Paul told us that they who live godly in Christ Jesus shall suffer persecution. And Paul knew what he was talking about. He was beaten with rods; he was scourged; many stripes were laid on his back; he was shipwrecked and spent a day and a night in the deep; he had trouble from those who hated his doctrinal stand; he had trouble from brethren who misunderstood his zeal.

This was the beginning of conflicts for Samson. He was going to face many conflicts in the future. He was going ultimately to score some decisive victories over God's enemies, the Philistines. This incident reminds one of David who also fought a lion before he faced Goliath, the enemy of Israel. David was in a perennial battle. On the contrary, Solomon, David's son, had it easy. He sat on a comfortable throne and the sun shone upon him, and it seems that he breezed through without the conflicts that characterized his father David. And yet this prosperity submerged Solomon into a quagmire of sins and iniquities.

Jesus, our blessed Savior, faced the devil. You recall, after Jesus' baptism, he was led into the wilderness. There for forty days and forty nights he confronted conflicts that sought to shatter his mission and ministry. And yet Jesus emerged the conqueror; he used the Word of God. He defeated the devil with three verses from Deuteronomy. We can also be victorious. The devil need not destroy our testimony and influence. And if Jesus could do it with three verses from that difficult Old Testament book, we can do it with the whole Bible. We have access to all of the promises, examples, and exhortations. And we too can win the victory over the world, the flesh, and the devil.

The Apostle Paul informed us that life was going to be a fight. In Ephesians 6 he reminded us to put on the whole armor of God—to wear the helmet of salvation—and the breastplate of righteousness, and to carry the shield of faith and the sword of the Spirit. In other words, we are going to a battle, not a banquet; we are going to a fight, not a feast. So many Christians have the idea that because their names are written in heaven, and they have become members of the family of God, they should be exempt from the trials and the fiery temptations that assail others. Not so. In fact, persecutions may proliferate after we are saved. I know that when I accepted Christ, I landed immediately in the midst of parents and kinfolks who thought that I had done wrong because I had changed denominations. It had been easier for me to remain unsaved, for the moment I received Christ, the devil opened up his battery of opposition and made life miserable. But the strength I received from those encounters has served me well in later years. I wouldn't have missed the opposition for anything.

Samson faced a fierce problem here at the beginning. This lion was called a "young lion" in the contest. This doesn't mean that he was a beginner or inexperienced. The emphasis here in the Hebrew is that he was strong and hungry. So at the beginning, difficult trials may come to Christians, as in my case. Some of you who are reading may be facing serious ordeals—young lions, if you please. But remember that Samson faced a terrible problem to begin with. Troubles and trials are not graduated. They do not come slowly and then grow in intensity; the terrible storm often comes at the beginning. So it was in the case of this young man.

And notice that Samson was not prepared for this ordeal. He was on a different mission. He was looking for a wife, not a young lion. The Scriptures state that when he faced the lion, he had nothing in his hand (Judg. 14:6). He had no sword or spear with which to fight the assailant. I look back upon my own experience when my parents and relatives opposed the move I had taken when I received Christ. I felt so defenseless. I look back now and wonder how I withstood parental attacks. I had no experience. By nature, I was a shy little guy. I had no power of rhetoric or logic to contradict the wave of opposition. I had barely begun to read the Bible and I was not conversant with the many resources available to the believer in the hour of conflict. But I stood firm, and God gave me the victory. I had to lean wholly on him because I had no resources of my own. I had to stand still and see the salvation of the Lord.

And notice that Samson was alone. There is strength in companionship. Yes, there is mutual encouragement when someone else is there. But he was alone; he was not prepared to face this contingency. The devil often makes his best inroads into our lives when we are alone. Watch the hour of solitude. Be careful when aloneness invades. You recall that Eve was alone when the devil attacked her. Where was Adam? He should have been home with his wife. Jesus was alone when the devil attacked him in Matthew 4; where were Peter, James, and John? He trod the winepress alone. Even on the cross, he cried, "My God, my God, why hast thou forsaken me?"

But notice that the Spirit of God came on him. This is how to win the victory. The weapons of our warfare are not enough; we need the unseen power of the Holy Spirit. No wonder that wonderful verse in 1 John 4:4 is so true, "Greater is he that is in you, than he that is in the world." We cannot run from the devil. He runs faster than we. We cannot use our weapons because we have none. Our own abilities are not sufficient. We must rely upon Christ. That explains the victory in my case; I cannot explain it any other way. In my own natural ability I could not have withstood the bombardment of problems that assailed me in my home and from other sources when I received Christ. But in retrospect, I can recognize the power of the Holy Spirit at work; I can recall the hand of God rising to my defense. And so must we rely on that strength from above in the hour of trial and temptation. In our own selves, we are not equal to the problems that surround us. We are not wrestling against flesh and blood, but against principalities and powers and spiritual wickedness in high places.

II. The Confections of the Christian Life

But if the Christian life contains struggle and hardship, it also provides "joy unspeakable and full of glory," and blessings that make the struggles minimal in comparison. After his victory Samson found honey in the carcass of the lion, and he ate some of it. The blessings of the Christian life are innumerable. They are like the starry heavens that Abraham surveyed when God promised him a seed as numerous as the stars in the vast expanse above him. I look back across these years of living for Christ, and I stand amazed in the presence of blessings beyond number. From the familial struggle came my call to preach two months after my conversion. My mother, brothers, and sisters—all the family except my father—attended that first service. When I extended the invitation, my little mother was the first one to respond to the invitation. Honey! Then every member of my family, two brothers and two sisters, received Christ in the same service. More honey! Twenty-five others were saved that night. Still more honey! Oh, the sweet joy of living for Jesus.

One of the great blessings of the Christian life is the knowledge that our sins are forgiven, not only our past sins, but our future sins as well. God does not save us from the point that we accept him back to our birth. I believe that the moment we accept him, he forgives our sins from birth to death.

Another confection of the Christian life is the daily companionship of Christ. It is wonderful to know that in our journey the Savior has promised to be our daily companion. He will never leave us nor forsake us, he promised that he would be with us even unto the end of the age; he is a friend that sticks closer than a brother. No human being, no matter how much he may love us, can guarantee his constant presence. There are areas where human beings cannot go. Think of it, we are never alone. In every crisis of life, he who is the author and the finisher of our faith is always there to give us, not the spirit of fear, but the spirit of peace and a sound mind. So let the storms of life descend. Let the winds blow. Let the storms surround us. The Master of life and death is in our corner.

You recall that in the Twenty-third Psalm, David affirmed this confronting truth, that "in the valley of the shadow of death, thou art with me." Notice, he did not write "thou art *for* me," because the Lord does not operate our lives by remote control. He does not sit placidly in the heavens and send us long-distance messages, "Go to it down there. I am for you—I am pulling for you." No, he is *with* us! Down here in the midst of our turmoil and despair, down here where we weep and our hearts are broken, down here where loved ones die and sickness devastates, he has promised to be with us. The "process theologians" have done a great service to theology, Whitehead, Hartshorne, and others, by affirming the contemporary nature of God. He cares for the present. He is not only a God of yesterday and tomorrow, but he is existential. He is willing to help me in the present and to minister to my daily needs. With a Savior like that, I can face the turbulent hours that lie before me.

Another confection of the Christian life is the promise of heaven beyond death. This is not an empty dream or a wish projection. Jesus declared, "If it were not so, I would have told you." This perfect environment which lies before us should motivate us to serve the Lord and love men in this present evil world. Think of it, we are going to a place where there are no sorrows, no tears, no funerals, no farewells. But heaven is a prepared place for a prepared people, and the preparation is to accept Christ as personal Savior; it is just that simple. Of course, once this indespensable moment happens in our lives, we spend the rest of our days loving Jesus, serving him, doing his will, and sharing him with others.

No wonder Paul could say "to live is Christ, and to die is gain." We never lose anyone who goes to heaven. Do not tell people that you have lost a loved one if they are saved. I have a father and a brother in heaven. I never say I have lost them. I know where they are. People are not lost if you know where they are. The next time you talk about a departed Christian loved one, tell them that you *gained* your loved one. For people are more yours in heaven than they ever were down here. They are now beyond cancer, heartaches, tears, anxieties, and depressions. They have gone to be with Jesus, for to be absent from the body is to be present with the Lord.

And the overwhelming part about it is that we go there immediately at physical death. We do not wait until the judgment day or the resurrection. The dying thief went to heaven immediately. Christ told him, "Today, you will be with me in paradise." Today, not at the last day; today, not after the resurrection. What a promise! The moment my body dies, I am in the presence of Christ and in fellowship with the general assembly of the firstborn. Paul exulted that it was so beautiful he could not even put the transcendent glory into human words. In 1 Corinthians 12, the apostle took a trip to heaven, and he found it awe-inspiring.

III. The Commission of the Christian Life

We have talked about the conflicts of the Christian life, the lions that we encounter along the way. We have talked about the confections of the Christian life—the honey that we gather and enjoy. Now I move to the commission of the Christian life. When Samson found the honey in the carcass of the lion, he enjoyed it, but he began to think about his parents. They would enjoy the delicious honey; and so it is our duty to think of others, sharing with them the sweet grace of God. When I was saved, I wanted my mother, father, brothers, and sisters to know about this never-ending salvation that had become mine when I received Christ as Savior. My mother was the first convert, and my brothers and sisters also accepted Christ as Savior in my first sermon. It took us ten years to win my father, but he too came to accept the sweet forgiveness that only Christ can give.

The Christian religion must have a horizontal extension. We are not saved to become loners, or to hoard the grace of God. The joy we know in Christ and the peace that is ours because of his saving love should be shared. All around us are kinfolks and friends and neighbors who do not know the grace of God. Someone must take the honey to them. So God has saved us, not to sit, but to serve. And we have a marvelous commodity to dispense. What could be greater than to take the honey of God to hungry men and women? I am so glad that someone shared it with me, and it behooves me to extend the grace of God to those around me.

This is the unique work that Christians can do for Christ. The unsaved man can duplicate everything we do for Jesus except winning others and sharing God's grace. If we say we serve the Lord because we live right, the unsaved man can duplicate that. Many people who do not follow Christ have high moral standards and live clean lives. If we say we serve the Lord because we give of our money, many unsaved people are generous with their substance. I was in a church recently where an unsaved man donated fifty thousand dollars to the building fund! So the ungodly are often generous, even with religious causes. If we say we love the Lord because we are faithful in our attendance, many people who do not belong to the church attend with an astounding measure of regularity. In fact, some of them attend more faithfully than some of the church members who profess to be Christians. Recently, in a revival service the pastor pointed out a man who had been there every night and informed me that he was praying for his salvation. And he added that the man attended prayer meeting frequently, as well as Sunday services, although he was not a professing Christian. But when you reach out to win someone to Christ, you are doing something that the unsaved man cannot do. Winning others, and passing out the honey to others is the only unique work we can do for Christ.

And our sharing and serving should be done with humility. You will notice that the Scripture says that Samson shared this honey with his mother and father, but he did not tell them how or where he had found it. He could have bragged about the fight with the lion and the subsequent victory. But he desisted from bringing glory to himself. Sometimes, I wonder if some of us are not serving the Lord and doing great exploits so we can brag about it and inform others how spiritual we are. We are living in a day when divine healers have people to give their testimony, and tremendous publicity surrounds these so-called divine healings so that the healer, though he claims that the glory belongs to God, is put in the spotlight. Our job is to tell the world what the Lord has done for us; our job is not to tell the world what we have done for the Lord. The right kind of humility will make us say with Paul, "By the grace of God, I am what I am" (1 Cor. 15:10).

And sharing the grace of God, the honey of his love, is something that every Christian can do. Every believer cannot be a preacher or a singer or a teacher, but every child of God can share with others the sweetness of salvation. There is a sense in which every saved person is in full-time Christian service. God calls some into a specialized service, but he calls all to share with others the good news of the gospel. And you have an entree with someone that no one else has. I can win some that you cannot win, and you can win some that I cannot win. But every one of us needs to be busy; what a tremendous revival would erupt in the church if every believer became busy about this matter.

And if you stop to think about it, you are saved today because someone else shared with you. If I were to ask you to tell me just one thing, "Who was the person instrumental in winning you to Christ?" some of you would say it was a Sunday School teacher and others would say that it was a pastor. Others would testify it was an evangelist; someone else might mention that it was a parent, a mother or a father. But in every case, someone was the link between your life and the grace of God. So it behooves us to reciprocate; we should share with others even as someone shared with us.

In my case it was a next-door neighbor. This lovely lady was always inviting us to the Baptist church. We were devout Catholics, and we would refuse her invitation. But she persisted—she did not give up. She must have invited us twenty-five times and we refused. But one day she invited again, and here I stand today because of a friend who lived next door and would not eat the honey alone, but shared it with the people who lived next door. As a result of her persistence, I was saved and began preaching. My entire family was saved, and for almost five decades I have reached thousands in this country, all because of a next-door neighbor who brought us some honey.

10
Does Jesus Care?

Saul, Saul—(Acts 9:4)
Martha, Martha—(Luke 10:41)
Simon, Simon—(Luke 22:31)
O Jerusalem, Jerusalem—(Matthew 23:37)
My God, my God—(Matthew 27:46)

The Christ I know is concerned about the details of your life and mine. Many people think that God is so involved in the big things of the universe—the galaxies, the constellations, the laws of nature, the awesomeness of space—that he has no time to infiltrate the domain of our meager existence and feel with us and for us. This is incorrect because the mystery of his personality involves him in both the macroscopic and the microscopic. He is Lord of the infinite and also of the infinitesimal; he is beyond us and among us simultaneously. He is a High Priest who can be touched with the feeling of our infirmities.

One day Jesus was ministering to a pressing crowd. The multitudes were surging on every side. They wanted to hear what he said and see what he did. Unparalleled teachings were falling from his lips. Acts of healing were being witnessed on every side. In the midst of the jostling and the pushing, Christ stopped and asked, "Who touched me?" The disciples were perplexed. They informed the Master that everybody, in a sense, was touching him. But Jesus had not ignored a tender touch from a sick little woman. She had been ill for twelve years, and she thought, *if only I could touch the hem of his garment I will recover my health.* She pushed through the crowd and when she came near the Savior, she reached out with a trembling hand, white and wan from perennial bleeding, and stroked the hem of his robe. Instantly, she was healed, and Christ was not insensitive to her touch.

I have five texts for my sermon today. They all repeat a name twice. These are the only five verses where this double expression is found, and each one indicates Christ's concern for some area of living that corresponds with the needs of our day.

His Care for Sinners—"Saul, Saul"

Saul, who later became the Apostle Paul, was a diligent persecutor of the church. He had a brilliant mind and a passionate heart. But he had dedicated himself to the elimination of the early church. He was a Pharisee of the Pharisees, born of the stock of Israel, member of the tribe of Benjamin, a Hebrew of the Hebrews. But he despised Christians. He was intent on exterminating this newly organized sect, before it spread to others. He had done a thorough work of persecution in Jerusalem, and now he was going to Damascus to trouble the church there. As he approached the city, he saw a light, and he heard a voice that penetratingly asked, "Saul, Saul, why persecutest thou me?" This confrontation became the foundation for his salvation. He replied, "Lord, what wilt thou have me to do"? (Acts 9:6).

This was the point where he was saved. He was not saved three days later when Ananias baptized him; he was born again when he saw Christ and yielded to him. He corroborates this in 1 Corinthians 15:8. In this passage he is testifying to the reality of the resurrection of Christ, and after alluding to various witnesses who saw the risen Savior, he affirms, "And last of all he was seen of me also, as one born out of due time." In other words, Paul was saying that when he met Jesus on the road to Damascus, there and then he was born again. He did not deserve it, and later in verse 10 of the same chapter, he says that "by the grace of God, I am what I am." It always amazed Paul that Christ would save him. He called himself "the chief of sinners" (I Tim. 1:15).

So Jesus cares for you and me. No matter who you are or what you have done, the grace of God is bigger than your transgressions. No combination of human corruptions can baffle the grace of God. "Though your sins be as scarlet, they shall be as white as snow" (Isa. 1:18). Jesus paid it all, and when he died on Calvary, he expiated all of your sins. He paid for the sins that you have committed and for the sins that you are going to commit. Do not think that the Lord deals only with your past sins at the point of salvation. Never again will you be an unsaved person. When Christ died on the cross, He cried, "It is finished." Jesus did not do a halfway job with our salvation. He finished that work. "He that hath begun a good work in you shall perform it unto the day of Christ Jesus" (See Phil. 1:6). Your relationship to him is complete the moment that you accept him as your Savior.

Did you ever stop to realize that God owns the world? Every tree, every flower, every river, every sea, the stars in the heavens, and the formations of the earth beneath our feet are his. The psalmist told us: "The earth is the Lord's and the fulness thereof" (Ps. 24:1a). And yet, though he owns everything, he had to buy sinners! Unworthy sinners cost God a crucifixion! Jesus died for you and for me. God had to pay a price for us, though the whole universe belongs to him. That is why Paul wrote that we are not our own—we are bought with a price (I Cor. 6:19).

In the Old Testament, the Jew observed the sabbath as a sign of a covenant or a contract between God and him (Ex. 31:12-17). On that day the Israelite would rest to commemorate God's resting after creation. Now the believer observes Sunday as a sign that Jesus rested after he finished his work on the cross. The sabbath in the Old Testament commemorated the finished work of creation; the Lord's day, the first day of the week when he arose, commemorates the finished work of redemption. That is how Jesus cares. He did something about our sinful condition. We could not save ourselves, and so he went to a cross and did it for us. Paul never ceased to praise God for the fact of the atonement. He gloried in the cross. He did not glory in his education, in his roots, his Jewish heritage; he did not glory in his morality; he rejoiced in the finished work of Jesus. And, sinner, he cares for you, died for you, and rose for you. Why don't you accept him now?

II. His Concern for Saints—"Simon, Simon"

Jesus cares for his own. He has promised to accompany us from point salvation to point death. He will never leave us or forsake us, and when we face death he has promised to be with us. Simon Peter bragged that if all men forsook Jesus, he (Simon) would remain faithful. Jesus warned him of the fact that the devil was trying to curtail his effectiveness by this spirit of pride. Christ can see in us things that we cannot see in ourselves. He is concerned about the quality of our consecration because of what it can do to us and to others. You recall how Peter failed Christ in the courtyard, but the Savior restored him, forgave him, and let him preach the sermon on the day of Pentecost that brought so many converts into the church.

But let us not forget that the greatest weapon the devil uses to cripple good causes is a backslidden Christian. The devil's greatest weapon is not the night club, the gambling casino, or the town drunkard, but a believer who has lost his first love and grown cold. Christians who have quit coming to church, who have stopped reading their Bibles, who have become lazy about witnessing, who have ignored the demands of stewardship are hurting the cause of Christ. Christians who are pessimistic and who lack concern for a lost and dying world can do more to hurt the work of the church than outsiders who sin flagrantly.

His concern for us extends beyond speaking mere words of caution to us as we confront difficult situations. He is praying for us. He reminded Simon that he was praying for him, and what is true about Simon is true about you. He is praying for you. He is praying for you in your business, in your domestic situation, in your moral struggles, in your relationship to others. I thank God for the prayers of many friends, and these petitions are most helpful. I thank the Lord for the prayers of minister friends who often tell me that they remember my ministry in their intercession. I have a gracious Christian mother who knows how to bombard the gates of heaven with persistent prayer. But the greatest joy and comfort to me is to know that he who can save from the guttermost to the uttermost is sitting at the right hand of God the

Father making intercession for me.

The devil is interested in those who are serving the Lord, and Christ knows it. You recall that Satan led Judas to betray Christ, and now he was after Peter. In our verse, "Simon, Simon, Satan is trying to sift you as wheat," the wheat is referring to the disciple group. The devil was trying to separate Peter from the disciples like one fans chaff out of wheat. The devil had worked on Judas with his fan, and he had sifted him; he had gotten him out of the group by the use of his fan. Now he was working on Peter. Christ did not pray for Judas—Judas had never been truly saved. He joined the group thinking that Christ was going to become a political messiah and deliver Palestine from Roman bondage. He then thought that, in that new order, he, Judas, would be the treasurer, become responsible for vast sums of money, and fill a prominent position. But when he realized that Christ was going to build a spiritual kingdom, not a political one, he sold Christ for the price of a slave.

Jesus wanted Simon to be a rock; the devil wanted to make him chaff. Jesus is concerned about what we become. He has a special place in his kingdom for every one of us. Every believer is in fulltime Christian service. And while the Lord calls some to be evangelists or pastors or teachers, every child of God is an ambassador of Christ. Every one of us has been sent into a lost world to win people to Christ and to announce the power of amazing grace. Our pulpit may be the school room, the court room, the office, the road, the home; but we have a task to perform, and the devil would like to cancel out witness and diminish our effectiveness. And if you have ever tried to serve the Lord, who has a specific job for you, you have known the pressures and obstructions the devil has tried to impose.

Let us not forget that Simon stumbled anyway. He denied Christ, lied, and cursed in his betrayal of the Savior. But Jesus' concern did not end here. You recall how later, after the resurrection, Jesus cooked a breakfast for the disciples. After the meal he asked, "Simon, do you love me?" He asked him three times, not only because Simon had denied him three times, but because we learn by repetition. So Jesus wanted to teach his lesson well.

Simon was restored. So remember that Jesus is concerned about believers. He knows the pressures of this world and the pursuit of Satan who wants to make us chaff when Jesus wants to make us rock. But even if we fail, his concern pursues us into the hour of restoration.

III. He Cares for Our Service—"Martha, Martha"

Jesus was visiting in the home of Mary and Martha, the sisters of Lazarus, whom Christ raised from the dead. They were elated with the presence of the Lord, and they became busy doing things for him. But then Mary began to talk with him and to listen to his words. Martha became incensed. There was food to be cooked and served, and the table needed attention. Martha was busy with these secondary matters and rebuked her sister for sitting at the feet of Jesus.

But the Lord reprimanded Martha in our text; she was busy about minor matters. And this is the concern that Christ has for the service that Christians render to him. He wants first things first. Food can wait, material things can wait, the temporary things can wait, but Mary had chosen the better part, and so should we. I am sure the Lord in heaven is saddened with the major emphasis we place on secondary matters. We expend our energies on the passing and the transitory. Life is short, and we must not major on minors. We must not concentrate on and be troubled by things around us. The King's business requires our primary concern.

I am afraid that so many of us are weak at this point. We have the idea because we are *doing something* that we are pleasing the Lord. But we have not learned how to rearrange our priorities. It is possible to waste the days and hours on minor matters. It is easy to make some kind of activity a substitute for the main things that Christ would want us to do. As he talked to Martha, one can sense a tone of love, not just a harsh reproach. And he is like that; he knows how to rebuke us with tenderness. He does not break a bruised reed nor quench a smoking flax. He can be touched with the feeling of our infirmities. He is bone of our bone and flesh of our flesh. The Book of Hebrews explains that he did not choose to

DOES JESUS CARE?

come in the nature of angels, but rather of the seed of Abraham. So he knows our infirmities; he knows our tendencies; he knows that we are dust and prone to mistakes, even when we think that we are doing right.

The Word of God says that he sympathizes with us and he cares, even when we stray and are disobedient as believers. Hebrews 5:6 says that he is a priest forever after the order of Melchisedec. The writer did not say that Jesus was a priest forever after the order of Aaron. For Aaron and his priests could officiate only in the Temple. They were restricted as to locale. But Melchisedec met Abraham on the field of battle and blessed him there. So Christ can meet us on the field of battle—he is not confined to a place. Wherever we face our sternest conflicts, Christ is there to bless us and to help us. There is increasing conflict in this world; we fight battles in the home, in our business, in getting along with others. The Lord of hosts has promised to help us in the time of need. He does not help us by eliminating the conflicts, for these are a part of our freedom and also a part of our development. He strengthens in the inner man; he gives us inner power so we can confront the heartaches and sorrows that are going to be our experience during our journey in time.

Jesus, by his life and teachings, set an example of service, and we should follow in his steps. He was concerned for others; he loved and cared for people and saw in them a potential that awakened their inner powers when they came in contact with him. We should follow in his steps. We should imitate his example. The critics around the cross uttered a true evaluation about his concern. They yelled, "Others he saved. Himself he cannot save." And when he was dying on the cross, he asked the Father to forgive the people; they did not know what they were doing. When Beethoven wrote his stirring music, he did not compose it simply for admiration. He did not want people merely to look at the score and comment that it was beautiful and well-done. He wanted people to play the music, reproduce it, and inspire others by repeated performance. He was not looking for admiration; he wanted performance. So Jesus did not serve simply to inspire applause; he wants people to take his pattern of helping others and serving others and duplicate it. He said, "As the Father hath sent me, even so send I you." He said that he was "the light of the world," but then he turned to his own disciples and told them that they were to be "the lights of the world." He wants us to copy his pattern and example.

When the disciples were businessmen and fishing for fish, Christ came and offered a new challenge. He said, "I want you to become fishers of men. I want you to work with people and to expend your energy and abilities in service to others."

IV. He Cares for Society—"O, Jerusalem, Jerusalem"

Here we have Christ concerned about society, about our culture. He was not insensitive to the problems of cities. He was concerned about the individual primarily, but his sympathy and concern embrace the culture of mankind.

If you recall, Jerusalem and Palestine were under Roman bondage. The people wanted to break that yoke. One never understands the New Testament until he realizes the nationalism that was brewing in the heart of the Jew. When they saw and listened to Jesus, they thought that he might be their deliverer, their Messiah. But they were looking for a political messiah, one who would deliver them from the yoke of Rome. But Jesus did not come to build a physical kingdom, but a spiritual one. He taught them that his kingdom was not of this world. He wanted them to abandon their longing to revolt against Rome and to pursue a different course. He wanted them to let Rome defeat Rome; he wanted them to build a kingdom that would be here long after Rome and all earthly powers had passed away.

Jesus insisted that it was foolish to rebel against the strong Roman empire. In Luke 3:1-3 he pled with them to give up that foolish notion. He informed them that Rome would crush them if they rebelled against it. Some of the Galileans had tried to rebel, and Pilate slaughtered them, mingling their blood with their sacrifices. Then Christ warned them that if they did not repent, if they did not give up their ambition for a rebellion and change their attitude, that they would likewise perish. The word "perish" here is referring to physical death, and the word "repent" is addressed to the nation, not to an individual. This verse is not talking about salvation. Rather, it is referring to the Jews' desire to fight Rome and get out from under the yoke of bondage. Jesus warned them that they would be unsuccessful and would suffer great national loss.

Historically, you remember that in 70 AD, thirty-five years after Jesus ascended, the Jews tried the very thing Christ had warned them against; and Titus Vespasian, the Roman general, came and quelled the revolution, and a million Jews were slaughtered in that encounter. Now you can understand the meaning of that verse which described Jesus going to Golgotha, carrying the heavy cross. As he trudged along, women stood by the wayside and wept for him. But Jesus told these mothers to save their tears. He told them to save their weeping for their children, because the little ones who were tugging at their dresses on the Via Dolorosa would be the adults who would perish under Vespasian. The prophecy came true, and every nation and people that choose the way of the flesh, the way of materialism and humanism, shall perish. Jesus is concerned in our culture; he cares about the poverty that abounds in the ghettos; he cares about the crime that runs rampant in our streets. He cares about the wars that decimates the innocent. Oh, that we would listen to him weep for us as he wept for Jerusalem.

V. He Cares for Sin—"My God, My God"

This is the last of the double expressions used by the Savior, and it has to do with our sins. He was dying on the cross, and he who knew no sin became sin for us. As a result he experienced separation from God. These words are also found prophetically in Psalm 22. Some scholars contend that every dying Jew would quote Psalm 22, and that is why Jesus said it, and the reporters of the Gospels picked up only the first verse. But I believe it goes deeper than that. Jesus was suffering separation from God because he was dying for our sins. One Bible student contends that he repeated the phrase twice because he was addressing himself to God and to the Holy Spirit. But Jesus, in the moment of bearing our sins, suffered spiritual death. It was this death that saves us.

His physical death was a consummation of his spiritual death, and it laid the foundation for his physical resurrection.

The most expensive thing God ever did was to love the human race. It cost him a crucifixion. Creation, with its intricate design and its beautiful mystery, cost him a word. He spoke, and the universe, with its billion galaxies and its multitude of solar systems within each galaxy, was ushered into existence. But when it came time to save the human race, he could not merely speak a word; it cost him the death of his only begotten Son. We are not redeemed by corruptible things like silver and gold—we are redeemed by the precious blood of Christ. We are not our own; we are bought with a price. These words of Paul reveal the love of God and the expensiveness of sin.

The mystery of the atonement may baffle you, but we could never have been saved without the death of Christ. God requires perfection because he is a perfect God, but you don't have perfection, nor do I. We are all sinners; we are all imperfect; every one of us has sinned many times. You cannot pay for my sins; you cannot even pay for your own. I cannot pay for my sins for I am bankrupt and so are you. So Jesus came, and in the beauty of his sacrificial death, he took the sins of the entire human race on that Friday afternoon and paid for them. And now there is nothing against you. Don't let the devil tell you that you cannot be saved because you are not good enough, or you cannot hold out, or look at the miserable job that others are doing. That is not the issue. Your sins have been paid for! The issue is this: will you accept Christ and let his forgiving love make you forever a member of the family of God?

So Jesus broke down the wall of sin which separated mankind from God. And now no one goes to hell *for sin*; they go to hell because *they refuse* to go to heaven. Condemnation is an act of the will, not a mode of behavior. The unsaved man is not going to hell because he lies or steals or gets drunk. Jesus paid for his sins whether he accepts Christ or not. If the unsaved man went to hell for his sins, then God would be charging twice, and this would make *Him* unjust, and an unjust God is no God at all. If God charges Jesus on the cross for our sins and then charges the unsaved man for his sins in hell, God would be charging twice. Jesus paid it all. Unsaved friend, the sin bill has been paid. All you must do is to accept the gift of eternal life. After you are saved, the Lord will help you with your sins and weaknesses, but the first step is to "believe on the Lord Jesus Christ, and thou shalt be saved" (Acts 16:31).

Jesus died to give us life, eternal life, because this is a principle inherent in the universe. Life is built on death. Animals must die to become protein for our tables. Vegetables and fruits are wrested from their environment to become the foundation for our continuation. So as we live physically on the death of lower orders, so we live spiritually on the death of the highest order. "God was in Christ reconciling the world unto himself." "He was wounded for our transgressions, and he was bruised for our iniquities."

Accept him today.